FAUNA

CHRISTIANE VADNAIS
TRANSLATED BY PABLO STRAUSS

COACH HOUSE BOOKS, TORONTO

First English-language edition. Originally published as *Faunes* by Les Éditions Alto, 2018.

Coach House Books acknowledges the financial support of the Government of Canada. We are also grateful for generous assistance for our publishing program from the Canada Council for the Arts and the Ontario Arts Council. Coach House Books also acknowledges the support of the Government of Canada through the Canada Book Fund.

LIBRARY AND ARCHIVES CANADA CATALOGUING IN PUBLICATION

Title: Fauna / Christiane Vadnais ; translated by Pablo Strauss.
Other titles: Faunes. English
Names: Vadnais, Christiane, 1986- author. | Strauss, Pablo, translator.
Description: Short stories. | Translation of: Faunes.
Identifiers: Canadiana (print) 20200294830 | Canadiana (ebook) 20200294911 | ISBN 9781552454169 (softcover) | ISBN 9781770566552 (EPUB) | ISBN 9781770566569 (PDF)
Classification: LCC PS8643.A353 F3813 2020 | DDC C843/.6—dc23

Fauna is available as an ebook: ISBN 978 1 77056 655 2 (EPUB); 978 1 77056 656 9 (PDF)

I feel such a sense of solidarity with all living things that it does not matter to me where the individual begins and ends.

– Albert Einstein

The times change, and we change with them.

– Latin proverb

Just like their prehistoric ancestors, human beings still dream at night of epic fights with animals.

Between their sheets, they do not whisper secrets but instead hurl spearlike threats and murmur spells to summon every ounce of strength against their foes. Outstretched arms serve not to embrace the sleeping body at their side but to fend off wolves and bears, find shelter from the winds, carve a path through the storm. In darkness, all are plunged into a life-and-death battle against natural forces, a war without beginning or end.

To dream of a future where our species survives, we must get back to wilder times.

DILUVIUM

Even just a few kilometres from Shivering Heights there was no foretaste of apocalyptic weather, just a grey gloom and puffs of fog lapping at the car's headlights. As far as Agnes can see, vaporous white patches lie skulking on the ground. They look almost hungry, she thinks, checking her rear-view mirror. The car chugs along at a steady pace, piercing a wall of cloud that closes behind it like a curtain.

For a few moments now she's been so engrossed by these clouds she almost missed the sign for the Nordic spa. Yet they had clearly told her it would be hidden by the forest, scarcely visible from the road. She yanks the wheel, fearing she'll veer into a clump of trees, but her nails dig into the leather steering wheel and she comes to a stop in the middle of a clearing of gravel interspersed with yellow weeds.

There's only one other car in the lot. Bales of fog roll over its chassis and along the ground to the welcome centre, before tumbling down the steep slope to the foot of the mountain.

The dense fog engulfs Agnes's hands while she pulls her bag from the trunk. She came here straight from work, and regrets not putting on something more comfortable. Her high heels sink into the ground, where the leaves that have amassed lie rotting under steady rains. The surrounding forest is a tapestry of pine needles and soaked wood. A muffled roar hints at the steady, truculent flow of the river below.

Tendrils of cold creep under Agnes's clothing and skin and seem to burrow down to her skull.

In her raincoat pocket, her phone vibrates. The office can't live without her any more than she can without it. She'll have to turn off her phone. Gripping her bag tight to stay her shivering hand, she takes a deep breath like her therapist taught her, imagining a great wind of freedom blowing through her, from the inside out.

In the welcome centre, two women are in a heated argument. Behind them, massive windows like the walls of an aquarium magnify the forest below. Breaks in the cloud cover afford glimpses of small cabins and pools of a paranormal blue. Shrouded in shadow and mist, this landscape has a lugubrious charm. The arguing women ignore it. The taller one claims there's nothing to be done: the spa is closed, weather warning, torrential rains. In a raspy voice, the other, whose back is turned to Agnes, asserts her right to stay. Her shaking hands have a curious gleam in the chiaroscuro, as if wrapped in a watery film, or skin so thin and pale it lets a sliver of light shine through. At the sight of the newcomer, the women fall silent. Then the guest's face lights up.

'See! No one got your message!'

The owner doesn't back down. Every guest was informed of the closure the night before.

'But we're here now. You don't really expect us to postpone our vacations?' asks the young woman. She turns and winks at her new ally.

Taken aback, Agnes stares into the face of the stranger before her. Her features are youthful, symmetrical, and clean, except the pointed, chalky teeth set in her crooked smile. Her round eyes bulge. Her freckled skin seems to conceal nothing of what lies beneath, and on its surface beads of water shine, as if the vapours outside had condensed on her.

'I'm too tired to get back on the road,' Agnes concurs.

'See? We'll leave if the river overflows. Promise.'

The woman yanks the keys from the owner's hand and takes her new accomplice by the arm, like an old friend. Agnes notices her eyes: at once splendid and shallow, two small pools shimmering like tiny fireworks.

In Shivering Heights, life is an enigma of water and sky. Rain is frequent. Some days it falls in perfectly formed pearls or drops honed to a knife's point, leaving nothing visible beyond and no prospect of escape. But there is a peace of sorts at the heart of a downpour so precious and violent. On other days, the showers mist down like gossamer, enveloping forests and outcroppings, snouts and claws. Then the river gains the upper hand, forces mergers, annihilates the delicate invasiveness of the rains.

As Agnes and Heather, the stubborn young woman, sink into the scalding baths of the Nordic spa, the air begins to turn to rain. All around, in faraway mountains and up in tree branches and under the earth in warrens and dens, creatures great and small get ready for the coming downpour. The women are content to watch the fog twist and knot itself before their eyes, hiding and revealing snatches of landscape.

'I love water,' says Heather suddenly.

Though it's pointless, she paddles her arms like fins to stay in place.

'You'll see. We'll be completely new women after this,' she rasps.

Submerged in turquoise water in the middle of the mountains, Agnes still feels like the stagnant, lethargic woman she has become at work. She inhales, to take in the moment and hold it tightly in her lungs and stomach, but it seems to be constantly dissipating.

'Are you from around here?' she finally asks.

'Not really. You?'

'I needed to get far away. From work.'

A little laugh pierces the fog.

'You came to the right place. We're far away from everything, here.'

Heather's voice shifts strangely between deep and high-pitched, but she doesn't seem to care, and shoves her head under the water.

Agnes finds this young woman's forthrightness dizzying. Such lightness inhabits her every move, her very being, as she dives right into the shallowest section of the water and out again, and traverses the pool with the ease of an undine.

This might all seem less strange if Agnes weren't emerging from a drawn-out corporate restructuring. In recent months she's laid off so many people that their tears and sobs have come to seem more normal than the beatific, almost unsettling joy emanating from the bather beside her.

Truth be told, Agnes needs more than a week at the spa; it would take a thousand years of ablutions to rinse off the worries encrusting her body. Her muscles remain tense even as she sinks ever deeper into the hot water. All around her torso and her arms, small whirlpools live and die, leaving a wake of sparkling foam. Hot steam rises to caress her face. She'd like to fill herself up with emptiness, but she's breathing in less and less air, more and more water. Her skin drips with sweat and vapour.

When Agnes gets out of the water to head to her cabin, Heather follows, bent on further interaction. Soon, in Shivering Heights, two trembling shapes in Lycra bathing suits and flip-flops will make their way through massive clouds of fog. They'll tiptoe along, so small and alone next to the forest and mountains and river and upside-down abyss of the sky, the source of all this smoke.

The two women spend the following day in the spa's many pools, sweating or shivering, shedding dead skin. Without other guests to welcome, the owner leaves them to their own devices, then stops appearing altogether. Eager for new experiences, Heather slips into every bath, tries out the hammam and the sauna. Agnes becomes less disconcerted, learns to be still. Like the herons that sometimes come to rest in the spa in Shivering Heights, or the black bass riding the river's current, she'll drink, and eat, and wait, soaking wet, for the day to pass. Her muscles will relax; her breathing will slow down.

Little by little, the downpour smudges out the borders between spa and forest. In the afternoon, seams of muck seep down from the undergrowth in small furrows, extending their black tentacles into adjacent pools. Under cover of rainfall, Heather strips off her bikini top and throws it skyward. She swims easily, with precise strokes, but there is something forced about the way she stands: erect, shoulders thrust back, streaming water accentuating the contrast between her muscular body and soft, full breasts.

'Loosen up, Agnes. We're the only ones here.'

Heather lifts up her arms to redo her ponytail. As her chest thrusts out and lips part to reveal her small, pointy teeth, her wide-apart eyes gaze at Agnes, who looks away.

In Shivering Heights, the ambient humidity obscures vision. Drop by drop, it distills its musty aroma. Agnes reluctantly undoes her bikini straps and dives right back into breaststroke position. Heather's strange lightness is both seductive and somehow disconcerting.

'You have a great body,' she hears through the splashing.

Agnes wishes she could be left cold by the sight of Heather's dappled skin, whose suppleness accentuates her bone structure and musculature, or the athletic stomach scored by the thin, glistening line of a scar. But shivers run down her legs and arms. She suddenly feels an invasive presence in the cold water and another, even more sinister, beyond.

She grabs a towel and heads toward a distant yurt that's almost hidden by the trees. From the corner of her eye she sees Heather flapping in the water, then shedding the final patch of colour, her bikini bottom.

Occupied by even the most trivial things, the human mind can stay calm. That's what they say, or at any rate what Agnes's therapist believes. That's why she booked a stay at this spa. Stretched out in a hammock that encloses her like a cocoon, Agnes focuses on the crackling of the fire in the centre of the room, the squeals in the distance every time Heather is shocked by the steaming-hot pools or the icy cold river, and the points of light that dance inside her eyelids when they close.

After a few minutes, she falls asleep.

In her dream, Agnes is back in the fog. She sees ill-defined animal shapes, a forest of pinwheeling silhouettes brushing up against each other. Deer, foxes. Elongated creatures that are neither garter snakes nor worms emerge from the vaporous mass and slither off into the waters. She sees them swarming together in a writhing knot, a floating vipers' nest that morphs into a woman whose pale transparent skin reveals bones and veins and the blood circulating through her body. This infrared apparition opens its mouth unnaturally wide, exposing its skull. Agnes is drawn to the gaping chasm, as if pulled by a magnetic force she can't possibly resist toward this opening as wide as a storm drain. When her eyes open and her arms thrust out into the pitch dark where they find no hold, Agnes discerns that she has seen this girl's true nature.

A spasm runs over her body, then she wakes.

The ceiling above her is worn, cracked, water-spotted. When she gets out of the hammock, the woodsmoke makes her cough. She runs her fingers along the hammock's fabric and feels an honest roughness, a profound materiality.

Through the window she can see Heather singing to herself, draping a towel over her shoulder and putting on her flip-flops.

Above, the rainstorm marshals its forces.

That night Heather makes a meal of roots and berries, fragrant herbs, and other items foraged from the grounds. On the dining room's sole table she lays out a black mushroom stew, a tart earthy soup, and tiny whole fish with fire-blackened heads. She eats voraciously. Determined to relax, Agnes sits at the table and deliberately chases all thoughts from her mind. She has taken her time getting dressed, called her assistant, then turned off her phone again – for good this time, she is determined. With a few important matters dispatched, she can relax. Rest has brought on a new-found clarity, even as the edges of the world blur behind a curtain of rain.

'So,' asks Heather. 'Feel like a new woman?' A half-smile creeps over her pale face.

'I feel totally calm,' Agnes lies.

'Great. That calls for a celebration,' says Heather.

She bends over to get something from under the table, re-emerges with a bottle of red, drinks straight from the bottle, and passes it to Agnes.

In Shivering Heights, between four walls assailed by rain and wind, perched up among the blackbirds and the clouds, a woman breaks out laughing, and another shrugs and sips sour wine. Why not? Agnes feels a surge of guilt for not trusting her more. It might be no more than fatigue preventing her from taking Heather's innocent enthusiasm at face value. Under that soaked hair, behind that bran-flecked skin, there seems to course an unaffected joy.

Had Agnes even a dash of Heather's temperament, the corporate restructuring might have gone more smoothly. Perhaps the episode wouldn't have marked her so; maybe she wouldn't now find herself overwhelmed by lassitude.

'You're changing already,' Heather mumbles, sponging her lips with a gleaming hand. 'You're learning not to worry so much.'

The trust Agnes was coming to feel for her fellow guest is shaken. Heather leans forward. From her neck, a brackish smell, mud and chlorine. Outside, visibility is next to none; it's a chaos of water and forest and air, all jumbled together in the storm.

'Now you're ready for the end of the world,' the young woman says gravely.

Increasingly powerful rain pummels the windows with the fury of disoriented birds. Heather's bizarre eyes, twin sloughs on the hinterland of her face, do not blink.

Agnes's heart leaps.

Across from her, a hearty clanging laugh runs off its rails.

'You should see yourself. You're a nervous wreck!'

Agnes hesitates a moment, then lets a relieved laugh escape her lips. The tension in her shoulders falls away. Tonight, no matter what apocalyptic jokes and dreams of aquatic peril visit her, she wants to believe in her power to throw off not just this burden weighing down her shoulders but sensation altogether. She finishes her drink in one swig.

'Let's go to your room,' says Heather, waving a second bottle of red.

The rain soaks them so swiftly and fully that, once inside Agnes's cabin, they have no choice but to strip off their clothes and put on robes. The cloth clings to their skin. The humidity is inescapable. Little streams of water drip from their hair and down their backs. Inside, even the walls seem to sweat.

It might be the late hour or the intimate surroundings or fatigue, but Heather's irrepressible joy seems to have ebbed. She sits with Agnes on the floor. They drink their wine in silence. Outside, the rain keeps hammering down and the wind makes off with anything not firmly rooted to the ground.

'You look so sweet. I can hardly imagine you laying off all those people.'

The words come as Agnes is approaching total relaxation. But at the slightest mention of her work, she feels her fist clench and unclench, clench and unclench. It's as if her rebellious nervous system were performing her therapist's relaxation exercises, against her will. She closes her eyes. Her heartbeats can be felt in every part of her body, all the way down to the tips of her toes.

'You need something to take your mind off it,' says Heather, coming over.

Soon Agnes feels the faint touch of two wet lips on her skin, just in front of her ear. She starts, tenses up. But she lets Heather's hand slide across her stomach, into the folds of her robe, and come to rest on her thigh. The young woman kisses Agnes up and down her throat and jaw, then slowly works her way to her mouth. She tastes of alcohol and seaweed. Agnes's breathing quickens. Despite herself she feels her shoulders fall back and her chest rise up, untensed and weightless.

Heather straddles her thighs and holds them down in place, spreads the wings of Agnes's robe and runs her tongue along her breasts.

'Stop … Stop…' Agnes mumbles weakly.

Heather doesn't seem to hear, and presses her hand between Agnes's legs. 'You're already wet.'

Those eyes stare at her ravenously: two voids ready to swallow her whole. Heather doesn't stop; her fingers glide along Agnes's wet lips, seeking a way in, though she must be able to read the nausea on her face, sense the refusal in legs suddenly leaden. Heather seems oblivious to Agnes's unwillingness, or sees it as a challenge, like everything else. She smiles as she takes off her robe, and her eyes cloud over as her pubis inches toward Agnes's. She kisses her harder and harder, cinches her like a harness, urges her on with words that are drowned out by the storm.

Agnes is petrified, stilled by a deep torpor. She feels Heather not just leaning over her body but entering her veins, flowing through her bloodstream. She has no strength left to fight off this unchecked desire swallowing her whole. Soon not one particle of her will be left unpenetrated by this moist, avid being whose sweat and saliva and other fluids are spreading all over and inside her body.

When Heather orders her to lie down, Agnes complies despite herself. Her mind is already elsewhere, swept away by the rain hammering the cabin windows. A grey curtain obstructs the view; a dark aurora borealis descends over Shivering Heights.

The cracks in the ceiling drink in their moans.

～

Agnes wakes to the weight of damp sheets on numb limbs. Her tongue seems stuck to the roof of her mouth, and when she tries to get up a wave of nausea hits.

She gropes the floor around her and finds she is indeed alone.

The room spins. Despite her heavy head, unresponsive legs, and flesh that seems somehow drained of blood, she manages to get to her feet. A single purpose drives her: find her keys and get out of this place. Flee to the Border, and beyond. This lucid thought is not enough to chase the knot from her stomach, the nausea that has her reeling. The keys aren't on her dresser, or in her suitcase. Her coat pockets are empty.

Agnes vomits.

She flings on her clothes and opens the cabin door.

The flood surges in like the sea breaching a sinking ship. Agnes stands knee-deep in cold, dark, slimy water.

Outside, the storm has died down, the rain calmed. A grey sun crouches on the horizon. Somewhere in the forest a raven caws, but its sharp cry only emphasizes the deafening force of the torrent, the incessant raindrops on the floodwaters. The spa is underwater; the cedar cabins nearest the river submerged. Agnes fights her way to the welcome centre, which appears to float on the water's surface.

While she wades over, a cramp cleaves her stomach in two. Agnes can see that her car is no longer in the lot. She fights through water strewn with flotsam, surrounded by chips of wood and other debris swept up by the flood. She has lost all sense of which way to go.

Then Agnes sees Heather showering in the rain. She's naked, dripping dark streams, her body offered up to the elements. Her legs are stuck in mud as the rain cleanses her of sludge. She leans into the water to splash her arms, shoulders, and stomach. Her voice rises as she turns around; it is by turns husky and reedy. She is singing a tune whose finer points are lost to the wind.

A broad smile twists Heather's lips when she sees Agnes. She slowly waves a hand, illuminated in a spectral white that makes it seem almost transparent. Heather holds up a shiny object, then tosses it into the water.

A set of keys.

Agnes sinks into panic, spins around in its eddy. As she is swept back toward the spa, toward the most heavily flooded areas, she feels her heart rising in her throat. She is running, then swimming, until she once again reaches the river whose current, fed by torrential rains, has grown more powerful than ever.

The surge sweeps her away.

She is surrounded by the river's detritus, tonnes of dead leaves and branches, chaise longues and fence posts – all things accustomed, like Agnes, to resting on terra firma. Sharp objects slash her thighs, pieces of wood smack her from all sides, but only one thing matters. Get away. Get far away from Heather's voracious eyes, far away from the spa and the office, far away from all of it.

The waves upend Agnes and spin her around. Then, while raindrops harrow her stomach, while the world is swept away as the waters form a mighty river, a lake, an inland sea, her eardrums are pierced by the long shrieks that ring out on wet days in Shivering Heights.

CREATURAE

on't swim in the evening. Don't wash clothes after dusk. Don't travel overwater to visit your friends.

When lanterns fat as jellyfish burn above the boathome doors, and candles flicker in rows along sagging railings, the insects flitting around in the heat are bewitched by the light. Drawn by the glimmer of their bodies around the window, the birds of the sky and the nocturnal fish begin circling these dwellings built right on the water. The carnivores emerge; their predators soon follow.

Don't swim in the evening, the villagers say. The lights dancing like a bonfire are far too alluring, drawing the lake monsters from all sides.

It's a windless evening, a perfect night to be out on the water. Flames from the brazier rise up toward the stars, twisting between faces half-hidden by shadows. Hours have passed since the town stopped pitching and rolling, though Thomas hasn't noticed. His neighbours are earthsick. He twirls a skewer between two fingers. An eel is impaled on the tip. His heart is elsewhere.

Thomas's gleanings decorate the wharf: seashells and glass bottles and pennants cover the stains and knots in the wood. In the shimmering festive light, it's an almost elegant scene, a welcome worthy of Thomas's sister, who is back from the

Coast for a few days, with a friend. Every chair Thomas could borrow from neighbouring cabins has been set out for dining al fresco, and a nearby table has been laid with grilled fruits, fried larvae, and other delicacies. *I did my best*, he thinks, *but it's still not enough.*

At the wharf's edge, the whole village makes toasts to the prodigal daughter and to Laura, her friend from away. The pair have travelled a great distance from their school on the dryland to holiday here. From their clothing to their smiles to the coronae of flies above their perfumed hair, everything about these women proclaims their foreignness.

To Laura, say the villagers in chorus, raising their glasses. The newcomer lifts her cup, like a ship hoisting its standard before setting sail.

To Laura, Thomas says breathily, as his heart brims over.

The village has been cobbled together from old barges and sailboats, boards salvaged from yachts, whatever odds and ends the lake tossed up. From the sails of the ships that once plied these waters, the villagers have fashioned tents complete with living rooms and sleeping chambers. There is even a bar selling local grain alcohol alongside liquors imported from the Coast. Looking out from these dwellings, when the heat has broken and the mist has cleared, you can almost see the dryland, at the confluence of water and sky.

To people from away, the village looks like a squat, sprawling oil rig. Nothing could be further from the truth.

Walking the boardwalks reveals a world of bleached wood, rusty metal, and perpetually damp canvas. Precarious housing stands alongside gardenbarges where vegetables grow under broken-window mosaics. The decks are connected by treacherous rope walkways along which the village kids grapple, screeching like monkeys, on their way to school. On the west side are small craft of more recent manufacture, pleasure boats moored for the celebration. Discordant music emerges in bursts.

On a deck Thomas has painted a thousand times, only to see his work peel away under the waves and squalls, friends and family have gathered. Glasses shatter; laughter clashes; all around, people chatter and hum. Laura sits next to Thomas. She's smiling and frightfully relaxed. An earthy smell emanates from her hair. Girls like her – outlanders unfamiliar with their ways – rarely visit the village. The natural flow goes in the opposite direction, the one Thomas's sister chose. Not many stay here. The ones with rheumy eyes; the ones whose hips lurch no matter what they do; the ones whose dank toes harbour colonies of fungus.

Thomas lowers his eyes.

She'd never want to be with a local like him. If she could read his thoughts, she'd never take him sailing down the waterways to the Coast, to the cities, to that whole other world that doesn't pitch or yaw. Tormented by this thought, he completely forgets his eel. She reminds him. With slightly trembling hands, he breaks apart the blackened, crispy flesh and hands her a morsel that immediately disappears between beguiling lips.

Throughout the evening, Thomas introduces Laura to the guests pouring over from neighbouring decks. Cousin-this, friend-that. Without hesitation she kisses and hugs and explains. She's here for research. She goes to school with Thomas's sister. She's from the North. She has travelled several days to reach the shore of this vast lake, to find herself on this deck surrounded by rare birds and endemic species.

At these words, glasses clink, mouths laugh and speak in an unbroken stream. They sing the village's praises and comment on its habits of thought, wax lyrical on the art of grilling. The deck begins shaking from the music, in a concert of foot-tapping and savage yelps.

On the makeshift dance floor, Thomas shows Laura the basics: how to wriggle your arms like twin catfish; how to trundle-step like a fiend. With sweat steaming from her skin, she leaps, and laughs, and scrunches up her face. Performed by Laura, these awkward steps transcend mere local custom and are transfigured into the nuptial parade of some rare bird, the promise of another world shining in the black village night. She wriggles her arms like twin catfish; she trundle-steps like a delirious fiend. A world can be seen radiating out from her yellow eyes and narrow hips, a sweat-drenched world along her chest where mosquitoes alight.

With generous swigs of rum, Thomas had hoped to screw up his courage for a slow dance. He manages only to orbit Laura, adrift in her exotic scent. He'd give anything to be worthy of this woman, to surrender to his unchecked desire to flee this village and discover the splendours of the dryland. But his embarrassment over his permanently moist skin and his uncertain footsteps thwarts Thomas's attempts to move closer.

Surrounded by marine and avian life, the village at the centre of the lake is a nest of writhing appetites. On the deck, shoes clack on cracked boards, mouths sputter and pant, hips sway. It's as if the villagers' stomachs are bottomless pits, their legs spring-loaded dancing machines. You could almost believe that the moths whose flight captivates Laura are not insects but fairy godmothers sparkling in the oil-black night. It seems that this party will never end, that the villagers will remain forever in motion, spinning and jolting and waiting for a dawn that never deigns to show its red nose.

Only when a neighbour extends a hand toward the stranger, hoping to show her some new steps, does Thomas finally find it in himself to lead his partner off the dance floor.

The pair sit on the bench. Cigar smoke rises in curls above them. Nearby, card players are staking their honour, and losing. Fists pound the table. Two boys cling to the railing. Their game is to gobble down anything and everything the universe puts in their path: scrambled liquids, writhing insects, wormwood twigs they gnaw with gusto.

Side by side, with their noses in their drinks, Laura and Thomas feel like they're the only people in the world. Laura gazes at Thomas, eyes shiny from alcohol. He'd like to get down on his knees, travel up the byways of her body, tilt her head back and release a cry from her depths. But he's petrified. He asks about her job. She describes her lab and research missions, aquariums and graphs, petitions and campaigns. With extravagant hand gestures she talks and talks and talks some more, and he does his best not to hear. He never should have unleashed this torrent of ideas from her mouth. He knows villagers who have almost lost legs to the jaws of a freshwater shark, and others forced to fend off the birds to protect their catch of fish at the end of the day. It's not the pernicious intelligence of animals that needs protection but the people who dwell on this vast lake. It is he, Thomas: he needs Laura to take him away from this teetering existence, far away from his breeding pond; to hold him to her heart and take him away like a specimen fished from the water.

Rum-drunk, Laura suggests a swim. *We can't do that.* He reminds her in a whisper that the fish-filled waters surrounding the village are full of sharks. She's so new to this world. Sweeping away his warning with the back of her hand, she mutters something about old wives' tales. In the joyful glow of the lantern, she takes off her clothes.

Thomas finds a dark corner and does the same.

Their bodies tumble like deep-sea divers; they plunge into the black water, then rise to the surface, coming together halfway up. He pursues her past boathouses and shell-laden docks, swims between gardenbarges and fishing nets. Shadow puppets on tent walls gently light up the night and their path through the water. She dives effortlessly as a sea snake, and at regular intervals the water's surface is broken first by her shiny head of wet hair, then by the smooth, firm curve of her ass.

She stops in front of him and treads water. Laura's face now wears the very expression he has been dreaming of, but Thomas can't supress a wince when he feels the viscous side of a fish against his thigh. *Don't wreck this moment.* There she is, slowly paddling her arms to keep her shoulders and neck above water level, her face like a buoy. Small fears snap and pop in every muscle in Thomas's body. There are sparks in his fingers and legs, but he moves forward, unsure whether he most fears the menacing calmness of this water or the daunting proximity of such beauty.

Laura makes the first move. She brings her lips to his. Her kiss contains the chill of snow in the tropical heat, an immaculate wind awakening in him the desire to leave this place behind. They breathe as one. Their hands touch; their feet locate the improbable crest of a shoal. Underwater, she seeks out his thighs and hips and ass. Astounded by the texture of her skin, its purity in this murky water, he tries without success to lead her into the shadow of the platform, near the hulls. She finds her footing on the slick algae that populates the lake floor, as if it were the most mundane substrate, and clings to him, setting the pace, imposing her movements and rhythms and desires.

Her fingers slide under water, over his flank.

Though her face can't conceal her surprise, Laura's hand holds fast. Curiosity makes her linger over the hard, scaly skin, a patch that grows larger by the day, increasing Thomas's likeness to the other lake creatures. She palpates and then releases it, exploring its relief. A crease of concentration lines her forehead. She dives and stays under long enough to glimpse the silvery lustre of this patch of skin, then resurfaces. For a second her nail digs into his flesh – as if to take a sample – but the movement shifts into a caress. She runs her palm down the mark, measuring its size and shape, studying its form and sensitivity.

She draws him even closer, gives him a bright smile.

Don't swim in the evening. Don't wash clothes after dusk. Don't travel overwater to visit your friends.

Under the boathomes, hungry fish lie in wait. Others leap up to snap at the prey flitting above the water; a few enjoy the luxury of deep, dreamless sleep. All this nocturnal fauna blends together in a fog of pleasure and need. In the shadow of the dock, a shark undulating to the music of a faraway concert band slowly circles an embracing couple. The man shoots phospho-rescent semen into the water, then waltzes his partner around. In spite or because of the foreignness of these customs, she feels her whole body quake as she cries out.

The shark listens, feverishly arches its back, and continues its rapturous encircling.

Deep underwater, dark ribbons of seaweed sway back and forth, and the party's cast-off scraps swirl like confetti.

In the night, individual dreams melt into the collective reveries of species.

Mammals, birds, and reptiles circle back ceaselessly to devouring. Deep in sleep, the paws of cats and dogs shudder as they give perpetual chase. Sleeping birds and lizards reimagine the skittering of insects, the wriggling of fat worms, the fleeing of tiny prey, and the arrival of more voracious predators.

The origins of this game have been lost in the complex ramifications of evolution. Perhaps only when they reached this stable state of relative protection from danger did our ancestors feel a nocturnal life stirring within. Dreams took root in the warmth and safety of their first shelters, in the calm repose of the chaser rather than the chased.

Disaster films are born of comfort.

Despite their myriad triumphs, human beings still live their lives in fear of wild animals.

PANTHERA LEO

Under a toxic green moon, the mist crawls along the centre of the zoo's deserted walkways until it reaches the stands of trees and wraps itself around the trunks. In the animals' enclosures, ribbons of fog encircle them like straitjackets. Enshrouded, they appear and disappear like flickering ghosts.

A faraway river roars. The wind carries an aromatic scent of cedar, with pungent notes of leaves and insects rotting before they decompose under the snow.

Sole humanoid among the wolves, tigers, and crocodiles, Laura shudders. They've let her – a scientist hostile to captivity in all shapes and forms – inside, to fill in for the night guard. She has been issued keys to the cells, put in charge of the prison. Strange twist of irony aside, Laura has no reason to be on edge tonight. She pinches her nose and packs the lions' meat into a large pail, then follows the path to their den.

Eager to escape the smell of warm flesh, Laura walks quickly. The ambient fog recalls the spume of an invisible sea; it unfurls like bolts of cloth toward a single point. Primates lumber in circles around their cages, breathing slowly, eyes riveted to the sky.

When the zoo's director begged Laura to set up her lab here, she at first refused to work for an institution whose inmates grew depressed, committed self-harm, and wasted away. But the virulent strain of parasitism she was invited here to study got the better of her curiosity. She doesn't regret her decision. What is happening in Shivering Heights is unprecedented. The parasite is in the water and it is in the animals' stomachs too. Yet, since coming here, each time she takes these paths, she dreams only of opening every single cage and watching the small, screaming, voracious creatures flee in hordes.

It may be the animals' restlessness, or the proliferating mist, or the danger of the lunar emanations flooding the earth: tonight it feels as if the air itself is poised to burst.

Laura sets down her load of food beside the observation window.

The lions' den is a wide concrete half-cylinder dug out of the side of a hill. They've done their best to create an artificial savannah. The enclosure's age is apparent in the way the walls, besieged by rain and wind, are webbed with lichen-filled cracks. At ground level, the window affords exotic views replete with a whiff of danger. But the lions long ago stopped standing up and rushing the Plexiglas. They're now content to produce the occasional husk of a disinterested roar.

Tonight, faithful to habit, the male and female watch the night pass in apathetic melancholy. They've never had to hunt for food. These crown jewels of a fading menagerie have long ceased to find relief in the changeless view of the stars or the hope of liberation. If it weren't for the occasional breath swelling their throats, they could quite easily be mistaken for recumbent statues moulded from the same concrete as their enclosure.

Laura searches the ring of keys they gave her for the one that opens the metal fence. It's her job to place the meal in an antechamber, then let the lions in to eat.

Trying to find the light switch, she approaches the night light hanging from the wall. And that's when she sees them on the other side of the barrier, only partially visible between patches of fog.

A couple.

The man's elongated silhouette bleeds out of the scene's dark backdrop. Just a few metres from the wild animals, he crouches, arms outstretched like a runner at the starting blocks. The look of concentration on his face is so intense – those scrunched-up eyes, those trembling nostrils – he looks poised to leap up and scamper into a hole at any moment. But he is thin, so thin, like a bird plucked of its feathers.

Behind him, on the edge of the river-fed pond, a woman sits dangling her feet in the water. Laura could swear she is smiling in the dark.

For a moment nothing moves save the ribbons of fog. Then, in a languid motion, the lion rises to stand on its paws. Over the course of a few interminable seconds, he saunters over toward the man, swinging his hips. He sniffs the human's feet and licks them. Though his coat has grown mangy, a trace of innate strength remains; it's in his muscles and on display in every step he takes. He turns to stare at Laura. His citrene eyes are piercing yet desperately empty, like stones set in some inert material.

A muffled sound escapes the man's throat. Then the woman's voice rises up. It's hoarse, almost a croak, yet somehow soothing.

'C'mon, Ed, don't panic. We're alive, right?'

She stands up and moves into the spotlight of moon. In this noble light, her pale, almost ghostly skin looks luminescent. Her jeans and windbreaker suggest youth, but for some reason Laura can't pinpoint, this woman seems ageless.

Into this danger she calmly advances, taking even steps. Either these lions have no power over her or she doesn't believe they are capable of attacking. She walks toward her companion, leans on his trembling shoulders, whispers in his ear. He listens but shakes his head.

'I don't want to,' he says. 'I don't want to do this anymore. I quit.'

Then, without lifting her bony hands from the man's shoulders, the woman looks Laura square in the eye. Her eyes shimmer in the moonlight. They are set abnormally far apart, like twin scarabs on the sides of her face.

The man's desperate stare snaps Laura from her reverie. While there's no way for her to open the cage without the risk of setting the lions free, she could invite the captives to take refuge in the antechamber where she was supposed to lay out the meat. She pulls open the sliding door that will grant access, then steps out of her hiding spot.

'Come in here,' she says. 'I'll put the fence back, then let you out.'

As if sensing her meal slipping away, the lioness stands and begins pacing the perimeter of the pond. Her head sways. Laura is hesitant to toss the rations into the pen, unsure whether such a course would distract the lioness or awaken her carnivorous instincts.

Animated by a sudden hope, the one called Ed moves in the direction Laura ordered him. Each step is infinitely cautious.

Never once do his eyes leave the lions. He brings a hand to his heart. A cross-shaped pendant glistens in the moonlight. Ed worries the pendant, mumbles a few prayers, then coughs at length. He can't stop. She wonders what he did to find himself in this situation, then turns her gaze to the woman's pale face and thin lips exposing small, pointy teeth.

Reassured by the man's patient progress toward her, Laura is getting ready to turn around and call for help when she sees the woman's leg stretching out to trip him.

Intrigued, the lions prick their ears. Laura's heart races.

'What are you, insane?'

Ed has fallen to the ground and lost control of his voice. Above him, the woman is now brandishing a cellphone with its light on.

'I'm recording. We need proof. This is a miracle! Don't you see? We did it.'

Ed is sprawled out. She puts a foot on his chest. He coughs feebly. She films his face at first, and then slowly raises the screen toward the lions.

'Let me go.'

'"*Let me go*"? It was *your* idea to recreate all the miracles. Happy now? We're really doing it! Can't you feel the fire of the Lord burning inside you right this second?'

As if this thought had forced open a floodgate, a whoop of joy comes forth from deep within the woman's throat. Her laugh sounds like the cry of an animal crazed by the alignment of the stars. Ed tries to stand. She kicks him back down to the ground.

He lacks the strength to fight back. Ed is so thin. With a theatrical movement, the woman throws off her coat and shirt and sends them dancing in the wind.

'Look! They don't even want my meat. They don't want it!'

While the unnamed woman prances in a victory lap, Laura stands still. She's paralyzed, unable to tear her eyes from the body sprawled out in the mist. The lions, she thinks, will attack any moment. No less astounding than their lack of appetite is the fact that this prey entered the den of their own volition. Nothing moves but the delirious body of the woman dancing in the background. At last Laura sees five fingers move. They are dragged along the ground, then lifted to their owner's head, which gleams with pale blood. The man isn't dead. Laura punches in the emergency number with one hand, then runs uphill toward the water hose. If the animals attack, she'll try to push them back with a stream of water.

'I'm here with you, Ed,' she yells. 'Help is on the way.'

Ed closes his eyes, palms open toward the sky, like a man who has laid down his weapons. He murmurs prayers while this witch struts around in the moonlight, swinging her hips, galvanized by her power. Laura endeavours to explain the situation to a stunned emergency dispatcher. The lions are possessed of a new-found vigour, apparent in their roars and their gait as they stride in a circle of diminishing circumference.

The awesome strength in their movements is ominous.

When she feels the threat approaching, the woman stops gallivanting. Concentration steals over her face. She walks toward the wall where she has left an oblong cloth bag and pulls out a hunting rifle.

Game on.

While Laura grips the hose, the wild animals spread their paws, ready to bound. The moment they pounce, Laura unleashes a jet of water, directed not at them but at the weapon threatening them. The unnamed woman falls onto the grass beside her gun. The lions flee the high-pressure stream and throw themselves on the easier prey: an injured man, still splayed out on the ground. The roaring lioness assails Ed with the same blows her ancient forbears unleashed on Christians tossed into the arena. *Panthera leo* has paws covered in hair fine enough to detect the most delicate vibrations in the soil, yet can shatter its victims' bones in a single blow. The faint sound of a fearful human groan is short-lived. So this is the fate escaped by Blandina the martyr and Daniel in the lions' den: to be torn from limb to limb by these very claws, these jaws, these muscles that evolution has sculpted and conserved unchanged in coliseums and safaris and zoos and other structures that will seem as strange to future archaeologists as they felt natural to their visitors.

Although this feline strength has grown sluggish from captivity, fog, and northern sun, Ed is powerless to resist it.

Nor can Laura, training the jet of water on the animals, dissuade them from their hunt. It's too late. And while the lions rend their prey, the soaked young woman runs toward the antechamber where Laura had planned to leave the great cats' rations. The woman wants out.

Laura hesitates, then walks toward the metal fence. In the distance, sirens wail. The woman seizes the bars, rattles them like a prisoner – as if it wasn't she who sentenced Ed to death. When Laura enters her field of vision, the woman stares intently. Her breathing is furious. Up close, her whiteness is all the more striking; she's the colour of haddock, splattered with freckles. Water drips from her hair.

'Help me,' she begs in a single breath, as if she can sense the hesitation in the way Laura's hands are drawing together.

She pushes her own soaked hands between the bars of the cage. Her fingernails shimmer in the moonlight.

The moment the key turns in the lock, she slams the door into her rescuer and flees without looking back. As the ambulance's red lights sweep the enclosure and the rumbling of police cars grows louder, she is no more than a shadow at the forest's edge. Before slipping away toward the river, she turns. Laura thinks she sees the woman's shimmering hand waving in the darkness. A winking goodbye. Then, in a fraction of a second, the fog engulfs the unknown woman. When the police and paramedics enter the lions' den with stretchers and hypodermic rifles, nothing is left of her but a windbreaker – perhaps left behind by another visitor? – and the sense of horror hanging over the park.

Once they've wrapped Laura in a blanket and made sure she has no bodily harm – her mind will be another story – it's her turn to enter the arena. The action is centred on Ed's dead body. In the background, fading into darkness, the still bodies of the wild beasts blend into the blackness. They collapsed when the first darts hit. Their eyes are sealed. From up close she can see their long eyelashes, their gracious blood-smeared noses, their heads thrown back with abandon. They are guilty of nothing, she thinks, as she pulls tight the silver cape meant to protect her from the cold. For the first time since meeting these lions, she pets their flanks. It makes her shiver, more than patrolling the zoo at night, more than the fog and the green moon, more than the anonymous expressions of the police officers. Their fur rises and falls to the rhythm of a long, deep breath, while Laura weeps gently and silently.

She is relieved they are alive.

The winter's first snowflakes fall over Shivering Heights. They melt without a trace. When the snow disappears, it's like it's crossing the threshold of the ground's frozen surface to keep going deeper down into the earth's secret catacombs.

On the big-cat observation bench, Laura reads the local paper. The events have the city in a stir: a citizens' group is decrying the lack of safety, calling on the city to close the zoo. The animal rights groups go further. A two-page feature explores Ed's online activity in religious forums. He had told people, in confidence, that the doctors had given him only weeks to live before the cancer took his life. There is no mention of the woman.

Laura puts the newspaper down. Behind their enclosure's glass walls, the lions await a transfer, or the needle prick that will signal their final departure. Their life hasn't changed. They sleep all day and night; they eat; with golden eyes like a candle's dying flame, they survey the monotonous surface of their enclosure. It's as if they have been held captive in their arena since ancient times and will remain captive *ad vitam æternam*. But perhaps they still feel wonder when the snowflakes tickle their uplifted muzzles. And just maybe, when their eyes are closed, they dream of pouncing once again.

Given what people are saying in the bars downtown, there's little doubt the lions will end up in the dumpsters near the zoo entrance, forgotten corpses in the heaps of dust, grime, and used tissues.

'I won't let them do it,' she tells the cats as she approaches the window.

But Laura knows she's lying. She has no intention of remaining in the area. The night before, the police teased out inconsistencies. Her story is never exactly the same, her actions and motivations never totally clear or comprehensible. She'll find somewhere else to pursue her research. She'll take along her specimens of the parasite and the data she has collected. Perhaps she'll spend some time in that village on the lake where she's always so warmly welcomed. Before she leaves, she'll ask them to use treated water instead of river water for the lions' drinking trough; it has crossed her mind that the parasite may be responsible for the lions' dulled reflexes when presented with serviceable prey.

She so wants them to have a future.

When the wind is fragrant with the ancient scent of trees, and the wild animals yawn and circle as their forbears have from time immemorial, Laura fingers the cracks that line their enclosure. Not even concrete is forever. The lions' den, like the coliseums, is weakening under the insistent pressures of cold, and humidity, and time, trembling imperceptibly.

VIVARIUM

'Laura?'

Dripping with muddy water, Thomas coughs as if his lungs were being scorched by the air. He's curled up in a ball on the deck of the boathome, clenching his fists and knees and flexing every muscle in his body. The sharks haven't ripped off any limbs; no part of him has been devoured. He's all there, intact. As he catches his breath, he has one sole concern. He has to find Laura. He has to find Laura in the same intact state.

Laura, his migratory lover, came back with the summer once again. But she's nowhere to be found. Lost. Not one of the eyes trained on Thomas in this crowd pulses with that yellow light. All these half-veiled figures in the fog are surprised to find him alive after his midnight swim.

Laura hasn't resurfaced.

'Out of the way!'

Like a feisty poisonous eel, Thomas wriggles along the deck, through the feet blocking his way. The planks scrape his sides and elbows. His constant coughing slows his progress. Then, freed from the viselike crush of bystanders, he recovers his footing and pulls himself upright. He makes it to the rail and stares out at the shimmering surface of the water. Nothing. Small waves break evenly against the hulls of boathomes, without offering up so much as a hair ribbon. As far as he can see, the lake's surface conceals only its own depths, not a drowned woman consumed by its waters.

'Laura!'

Thomas yells her name as loudly as his oppressed chest permits. He doesn't wait for an answer. She must be somewhere – clinging to some other deck, washed up somewhere. He runs over to the first sailboat and is lowering it into the water when he feels a hand coming to rest on his shoulder.

'What are you doing, my friend?'

For a moment, he actually thought she might be back. He almost believed he could feel her warm breath, with its sweet scent of mint and sugary alcohol.

'I'm going to find Laura! Let me go!'

Behind him, the clutch of partiers looks on, full of pity.

'What's going on?'

An awkward silence descends. Echoes of music and dancing still ring out from the boathomes farther out on the water. A glass hits the deck and shatters, tinkling ominously.

'What's going on?' he asks again, more worried than ever before in his life.

A woman speaks at last. Her voice is soft, otherworldly, unbearable as a siren's song.

'Honey, there's no Laura here.'

He feels a throb in his chest. A little to the left this time, where his blood has stopped circulating.

❧

Day manifests first as a light in the pink hue of the entrails of a gutted fish. Like every dawn, this one casts a pall over what's left of the party: abandoned half-empty glasses, tangled garlands, empty chairs arranged in circles for a meeting of ghosts. Here and there the smell of rum rises from the glasses. A gull pecks at a plate of leftovers. The music and dancing have died away. Under a few tents, couples come together for one last gasp before they too fall into deep sleep.

Away from the others on the end of the dock, Thomas offers up his toes to the sharks or whatever other terrors these depths can muster. He mixes dregs to concoct a drink that will do the job: warm his throat, warp his mind. He has searched everywhere for Laura, from the dancefloors to the abandoned hulks to the surface of the black water. She has disappeared, vanished, is nowhere to be found. Everyone he questions returns the same answer: *There's no Laura here*. As if she had never come back; as if they hadn't braved the sharks together once, twice, a hundred times before. As if she has gone away and taken every memory with her, save in Thomas's mind, where she swims these waters still. He's been searching for hours, moving in slow motion but turning up no trace of her passage: not a footprint, not one article of clothing left behind under a bench, no hint of her scent in the folds of a towel. She's gone. Yet he feels her presence still, crackling like static all over his body.

While the sky turns from black to pink, then fades from pink to grey, Thomas stretches out on the deck and stares at the clouds. Their shapes are desperately free, abstract. He closes his eyes: legions of crustaceans and molluscs shoal percussively around him, escorting his thoughts into the waters of the infamous man-eating sharks, unflappable creatures with pinhead-sized eyes. He's seen them before.

His loss is pushing him under, gathering furious momentum.

Time passes. No sea monster has deigned to nip at the feet he dangles underwater. When the clouds begin their descent, a bearded giant with arms thick as lifebuoys disrupts Thomas's solitude to heave garbage bags into the lake. Thomas would like nothing better than to be a ballast for these sacks of trash, to dive in among the roiling waste as it makes its way slowly to the bottom of the lake. He wants only to decompose with this garbage. But this garbage will endure for centuries, as Laura would have pointed out. Laura, his sea dragon, his *rara avis*.

His sunken treasure.

❦

In the days following Laura's disappearance, Thomas keeps coming back to the garbage dock. There, no one stops by to reproach him for this phantom sweetheart; no commiserating hand is laid on his shoulder with that tenderness reserved for the insane. Perhaps drawn by edible items of garbage, thick schools of fat fish keep him company.

His bucket fills up with fish each day. Sometimes his catch includes objects cast away by the villagers, and then Thomas's pulse begins to race: Could that be her tank top he sees in the grey morning? Will he one day fish out her black plastic sandals? No. The disappointment that follows each catch proves as deflating as the initial tug on his heart was thrilling. He flings each piece of garbage in a gliding arc back into the water.

To the garbagemen who send their bags dancing through the air into the middle of the lake, he makes it clear that he will make no conversation. His silence is addressed to all and sundry, neighbours and partiers whose looks all seem to say: *This guy reminds me of someone. Who is it again? Oh right, that weird guy searching for his girlfriend. The spooky guy.* Once his fishing is done for the day, he hastens back to his room and locks himself in. He scours his laundry baskets for some trace of Laura, sifts through the photos of his sister who moved to the Coast. In the shadows on the walls of his tent, he imagines a silhouette awkwardly dancing, raising slender fingers skyward.

Before Laura came into his life, Thomas had ceased to see the lake under his feet. Its protean form – gleaming or tumultuous, generous or covetous – had always been there, cradling his every footstep, marking his nights to the time of the lapping waves. Over the years, boathomes have moored to the docks and unmoored again, and the birds of the sky and the creatures of the deep have come and gone in the placid eternal return of migration. Then she showed up, in a halo of continental dust. His fishing nets grew heavy; the wind became a shriek in his ear.

The village's steady rhythms ceased to bring him peace of mind.

Every morning now Thomas takes the waterway from his room to the dock. And every afternoon he takes it again, from the dock to his room. In the most profound solitude, he rows and then swims – and there, under the boathomes, among shoals of mussels, he laps up the murky water to savour the taste of her mouth. As he moves beyond the gardenbarges, he tries to reconstruct what happened in the lake that night before Laura disappeared. But his memories are foggy. He can no longer say whether a shark's flank sent them into a panic or an overthrottled outboard motor threw them off balance, nor can he recall at what point he found himself alone, or even whether Laura dove with him recently. Every night in his dreams he finds her again, just as she was before, and every morning he must again puzzle out the events that led to her disappearance.

These gaps in his memory make his head ache.

He opens and closes his eyelids. She was there; then she wasn't. Now she's gone. She was there. Now she's gone forever.

That night Thomas wends his way through the crowd of dancers. His eye is drawn to the clodhoppers, the ones whose steps are a tangled mess. But nowhere on this dance floor does he find the white skin or yellow eyes or blond hair he is looking for. Laura isn't at the bar. Isn't in the tent. Won't be found hiding under any bench or poker table. He captures the attention of the partiers, meaning to ask whether they may by chance have seen a lost tourist. Strangely, whenever the time comes to ask this question, his voice weakens slightly. His jaw opens, his lips move, but all that comes out is subaqueous silence.

He decides to go back into the lake. Eases in slowly and soundlessly. The water seems colder than usual. He starts pumping his legs and arms, looking all around for her, examining the spume shimmering in the lights of the celebration. She's not there.

Methodically search every section of the village, he thinks. *Scrutinize every vessel and dock, look above and below every raft. Turn it upside down until you find what you're looking for. That's what Laura would have said.*

While the party rages on above him – effervescent, bright, and loud – Thomas searches through the tangle of seaweed and nets from the other side of the world, holding his breath for minutes and hours on end. She's neither here nor there. He gropes his way through the black water. The villagers who see him rounding the side of a wharf, or disappearing behind the hull of a boat, or diving deep into the lake, mistake him for a shark or some nocturnal marine mammal.

They point at him.

'Oh my God! Did you see that?'

'Yes, dear. He acts like this every time that girl leaves. He's searching for her.'

He dives and dives again. As the observers walk away, his dorsal fin gleams gold in the light of the moon.

Then the waves swallow him up.

IN VIVO

Species inquirenda, she thinks, observing the specimen on the dissection tray. Approximately sixty centimetres from head to tail. Its predators – or, more likely, its prey – must mistake it for a rock lying on the seabed. Its storm-grey scales and the alarming amplitude of its jaw display the sinister grace of archaic species.

Its fins hug its body stiffly.

Laura pricks herself on a sharp-tipped scale, and a pearl of blood forms on her finger.

In her memory, this specimen was longer and more slender when they brought it in the day before.

She turns on the fluorescent light above the counter, which brings every detail of the creature's physiognomy into relief. She could have sworn the curve of the mouth had been less pronounced, recalls a long, thin, stringlike shape. Unfortunately, there's no photograph for her to check against.

'Don't stay too late, Laura. They'll close the roads any minute now.'

The lab technician tilts his chin goodbye and points at the window before closing the door behind him. Tight clusters of snowflakes fall quickly down, blocking out the lingering dusk.

Sucking on her cut finger, Laura squirms on her bench and lets her shoes slide onto the floor. Her feet are swollen. Her intimate knowledge of coldwater life forms is no use: Laura knows no other creature with these incongruous features.

She puts on a pair of gloves, picks up a scalpel, and pierces its abdomen.

'You're going to tell me who you are, little monster.'

The dense red flesh is full of little bones. Laura carefully extracts the liver and intestines, then sets the skein of tissue on a different Petri dish. With a pair of pliers, she removes a scale. Its edges are smooth, its surface striated with concentric circles, the better to tell its age. The armoured plates appear darker and thicker than a moment ago, when she turned on the light. With a tape measure, she rechecks the specimen's length: fifty-four centimetres. A long wrinkle appears on Laura's forehead when she concentrates. She palpates, dissects, and analyzes the specimen. The stomach contains the same type of crustacean parasites found at the zoo. Laura sets these aside. The only sounds in the lab are the clicking of metal on glass and the quiet slurping of flesh being scraped.

Laura weighs and calculates, over and over. The numbers never match, always fail to add up. A headache nags her. She pays no mind to the blood pooling in her calves, or the energy welling up inside her, like sap in a tree.

With a distracted hand, she rubs her swollen belly and collates her data in preparation for a final stab at reconciling it.

Deep within her body, a *Homo sapiens* is writhing.

All through the evening the snow falls wild and thick, piling up in drifts that climb to the windowsills. The night seems inexhaustible.

Absorbed in her work, Laura doesn't see any of it. Only

one thing exists for her: this enigmatic mound of tissue, fluids, and silky organs. If this sample turns out to be the first one ever captured by a human, its brief, insignificant existence will take on capital importance. Laura doesn't notice her child kicking her in the abdomen. If she took off her lab coat, she'd be confronted with unnerving shapes pressing out against her skin, but her full attention is focused on the contents of her dissection tray.

A wave of gentle vertigo shakes her. No: this creature does not yet exist in the great tree of ichthyological classification. That plump fleshy mouth like a badly healed wound, this carnassial dentition – neither has been seen before. This creature's astonishing anatomy is unfathomable to her. Its skin appears to have been eaten away by cleaning products, its fins are long and transparent. Even a few short minutes ago it seemed fatter – too big, say, to creep into a basement through a cracked foundation.

Laura is trying to photograph the creature when every light in the lab suddenly crackles and then dies. The lab goes silent. Gone are the humming of computers and the gurgling of the pump in her colleagues' aquarium and the purring of the refrigerators where specimens lie in rows, straight and docile as corpses in a morgue. Only thin beams of moonlight illuminate the room. In the adjacent hallway, the emergency lights come on.

Laura stops and closes her eyes. She crosses her fingers in the hope that this power outage won't last more than a few seconds.

All around her, dozens of stingrays, plaice, sculpin, hatchetfish, and black dogfish rest in closed cupboards, painstakingly measured, analyzed, photographed, labelled, and classified.

Normally Laura enjoys these moments alone in the lab, with its intoxicating odour of formalin and disinfectant. But tonight, in this silent darkness, she can't help perceiving that thing she has only ever wanted to ignore. At regular intervals, contractions shoot through her body.

This was supposed to happen later, when she was ready. As of today, there were at least three weeks left on the calendar: three weeks to finish her work, prepare the nest, and await her future filled with tiny onesies and fluffy stuffed animals and pastel colours. Now she has no way to get home. Her car must already be buried in snow.

What are the odds of finding the most formidable *Osteich-thyes* she has seen in her career at the exact moment she'll be forced to leave the university. This is a once-in-a-lifetime opportunity. Especially since the specimen bears the parasite. If she cannot pursue her work, she'll have no choice but to let a colleague take it over, use her primary data, push her project forward.

What to do with this extraordinary catch on the table? She plugs the refrigerator into the emergency outlet, but there's no power there either. If this outage goes on too long, the specimen will be of little use, since the cold will escape the moment she opens the fridge door. She thinks a moment, then decides to fill a cooler with snow and place the body inside. If she pushes the specimen out the window, she could pick it up after the storm passes. But the moment she pushes on the window latch, wind and snow surge into the lab. As she kneels on the counter, Laura is buffeted, but manages not to fall down.

The cooler is too big for the opening in the window.

After several attempts, it becomes clear that it will never squeeze through, no matter what angle she tries. She decides to abandon the operation, but the half-open window won't budge.

Laura is trembling now. No matter how hard she pulls on the handle, nothing changes. Her uterus is contracting regularly, forcing her to work harder and harder. The cold and the snow keep pummelling her, as if settling a personal grievance. A glittering white drift forms on the counter.

Unable to push the pane back into the window frame, Laura can only stop the gap with her winter jacket and some lab coats. That keeps out the cold.

She grabs her phone and dials 911. The cooler and its precious contents sit out on the counter. At the other end of the line, a voice tells her they will do everything they can to send an ambulance. But the roads are closed. The weather is hampering the efforts of emergency services.

All she can do now is wait. Stretched out on the cot she keeps for long work nights and has reluctantly dragged out of the closet, Laura is in pain. Her belly is swollen like the sea after a storm as she sinks into the springs of the narrow cot.

Don't give in to your nerves, she tells herself. *Don't walk. Don't do anything liable to trigger labour. Like* Leptasterias polaris, *serene star of the ocean's depths, breathe deeply without moving.*

Driving away thoughts of the being lurking in the depths of her body, the creature she knows nothing about, Laura diligently counts off seconds between contractions.

For some strange reason, she has always sensed she would give birth alone. Thousands of animals do it every day, she tells herself by way of reassurance, all alone in mud burrows, in rainforests, or caves swarming with insects. Of course, this idea does nothing to calm her. She's ashamed to admit it, but she's afraid – has always been afraid – of childbirth. The entire process seems cruel and thankless. Rather than have the child grow in the shelter of her uterus, she would have preferred to spread her eggs, protect them, watch over them from a distance.

In dreams she has seen this child of hers. It is shaped like a deepwater fish, a monster curled up like a half-moon, waiting to emerge. When she woke up soaked in sweat, she saw her stomach not as a part of her own body but as the soft, pale shell around a foreign species.

With a little luck, this will be a false alarm.

She gets up to go to the bathroom and notices that the wind has blown out the bundle of coats she'd stuffed in the window opening. The snow's piling up higher – on the counter, on the floor, in the sinks. Outside the lab, the city has also been switched off. It lies like a dead body under the white gusts of the storm. Laura feels her head spinning. A powerful contraction immobilizes her, and then, with a ghostly slowness, she sets herself in motion.

In front of the bathroom door, she finds a trolley laden with spray bottles, rags, and garbage bags. The thought that another university employee might still be here, despite the extreme weather, fills Laura with hope. She glances inside. In the spotless mirrors, she sees the reflection of a woman washing her hands. She is tiny and bony, skin slackened with age, a far cry from the athletic students fed on organic vegetables who usually walk these halls.

Laura tries to make eye contact, to greet this other woman. When the janitor doesn't react, she walks over to her and touches her shoulder. Perhaps she is hard of hearing? In the mirror she catches the reflection of her own exhausted face.

That's when her water breaks.

Without embarrassment or empathy, the janitor stares at her wet pants, a hard spark in her eyes.

'I need help,' Laura says.

She feels about to collapse onto the floor. The anxious spasms running up and down her arms and legs are stronger than the repulsion she feels for this hostile woman with her icy stare. The old woman's dry lips are twisted into a malevolent smile that accentuates the length of her nose.

'What am I supposed to do about it?' she asks, as if the whole thing were a funny joke.

In the lab, the cold creeps through the open window in waves, like eels slithering through the gaps in the bundles of clothing. When she feels it, the janitor grumbles. Outside, the storm is ramping up. It's one of those winds that obeys no law but its own and can under no circumstances be contained. The moon and the city are rendered invisible; there is only a swath of black sky and millions of tiny snowflakes merging into a single entity. Laura scarcely has time to notice that her specimen is properly cold – it's hard to recognize as the same creature, so closely has it come to resemble the common silver redhorse, *Moxostoma anisurum* – when she feels, with her whole being, the compulsion to give birth in the water, to feel the aqueous flow engulf her stomach.

Laura instinctively approaches the aquarium. The fish are calmly swimming. Without a thought for the bacteria, she leans on the janitor's shoulder for balance. She places first one foot and then the other in the tank. The cold makes her shiver. Sitting on a bed of stones and algae, caressed by the viscous flanks of fish, she feels as if she'd never left that village on the lake where the women give birth aided only by their determination and insular tenacity. That was where, one appallingly hot night, this child took root. Tomorrow, best case, she'll try to save her research by hiding the disintegrating specimen in her fridge. For a moment she wonders if she has the strength to push a living being from her body, bring forth the unknown, face a power beyond her control.

The janitor lights a cigarette. In the middle of this snowy room, her silhouette appears even tinier, like a household fairy unimpressed by the unfolding catastrophe, destined to eternally repeat the same night with no thought for impromptu childbirth or the storm of the century. As soon as she butts out her cigarette, she starts clearing the counter and sweeping up the snow. She tidies and folds and rolls with a breathtaking efficiency. She cannot help herself.

The contractions grow increasingly painful. Laura surrenders to the pain with an ease that surprises even her. At the end of what feels like an eternity, she opens her eyes to find the lab has been cleaned up. There is almost no snow left on the floor or in the sinks. The open window is stuffed with a bundle of fabric.

Her specimen is nowhere to be seen. The old woman is leaning against the counter. She has found the stash of snacks in Laura's drawer and is munching on nuts.

'What did you do with the fish that was there?'

The janitor shrugs her shoulders.

'We have to find it!' Laura yells as she moves to stand, but a piercing pain stops her in her tracks. All she can do is slide back into the water and give in to the convulsions wracking her body. While every muscle in her body contracts, the janitor gathers her rags and disappears. Laura feels her head explode. She pushes. Outside, the weather takes a turn for the wild, like a voracious white animal with no heed for what happens far below the heavens.

Laura pushes. Soon the stranger will slip out from between her legs. The blood will unfurl like a flower in the water, blurring her view of the child she has allowed to borrow her body. At first she won't notice the unsettling agility with which her little one moves within the aquarium walls, how easily it glides through this cloudy water like an inland sea. Then, forcing herself to ignore her misgivings, she will plunge her hands into the water in search of the flesh of her species. She will hold out her palms toward her son.

In utero, the human child slips in and out of the fog of dreams.

Soon, as it sleeps it begins to flutter eyelids, smile, and beat its arms and legs. It dozes, undeterred by its mother's contractions, as she expels it from her stomach. Then it enters the outside world and leaves the arms of Morpheus.

For very young babies, the primitive dream state becomes a game of memory. The newborn discovers colours and movements and objects, then reproduces them in its sleep. Its parents' smiles and rebukes. The joys; the pains. The succession of everyday gestures. After a few years, the child starts imagining stories, characters who are friends.

Already a storyteller.

The more the human being grows, the more complex its dreams become. Images born of instinct are interlaced with the events unfolding with each passing second and the stories whispered in its ear.

INCISIVUS

They come out at night when the bedroom door is closed. First, the sound of a scratch – one only – like a signal from the leader: *coast is clear; come on in*. It makes no difference in what nook or cranny of the room or at what time this scout appears. A solemn performance unfolds, under furniture and inside cupboards and up against the walls. Cathy can't see them – how could she with her head buried under the comforter? They all breathe with the same rasping sound. Some nervously paw their surroundings, sharpen their claws on the floor, gnaw at the bedframe. She sometimes tries to locate them by focusing on a specific sound, but there's no sure way to isolate one from the others.

Tonight they're especially spirited, picking and scratching and slapping the ground with their hindpaws. From time to time you hear them make that same high-pitched sound that had accompanied their metamorphosis from grey rabbits to creatures of a ghostly white. Their squeals intensify, as if the earth were quaking and the air pressure plummeting. This has to stop, Cathy thinks. Her mind is a muddle. She rolls over in the sheets.

Sleep does not find Cathy until very late that night, in this room alive with the sounds of nibbling and mischief. These are nocturnal creatures. Morning, when it finally comes, is silent.

In the kitchen Cathy's mother greets her with a bowl of oatmeal and a glance of exasperation untempered by concern.

'Dreaming again?'

Cathy sullenly digs her spoon into her porridge. Her head is buzzing, her hands trembling from lack of sleep. Right, *dreaming*. We'll see what good it does her mother to deny their ghostly presence. Cathy stares at her bowl. Her cereal grows soggy in the milk. Ever since the Ogress murdered Cathy's rabbits, she's been haunted by the horrible memory of their paws in the stew. She cannot forget the explosive atmosphere that night. Her rabbits holding pride of place in the centre of the table, a bouquet of shrivelled bodies in the pot.

A waft of charred bacon sizzling in the frying pan nauseates her.

Alert to Cathy's disgust, the Ogress stares at her sarcastically, then lifts a strip of pork out of the pan. It drips with grease. She stuffs it in her mouth without breaking her stare.

Maybe their war was brewing long before this exchange of flinty stares. Did it start when her father crossed the Border with another woman? The first time Cathy got drunk? Or when her mother watched the river overflow its bed and understood her reign was coming to an end? One thing is certain: they have never gotten past that moment when the rabbit's flesh was cut from the bone, sliced up, and boiled. From that point on, they've barely spoken. Each is acutely aware of the animosity roiling in the other's stomach. After every meal, Cathy says she feels bloated, or has food poisoning, and runs to the bathroom to vomit. The Ogress hits back with ever meatier, greasier meals. Truth be told, they'd love nothing better than to fight it out, to each drag her foe's enfeebled body through the dust, as one parades trophies around the ring.

'This has to stop.'

The words have bubbled to the surface, unbidden, almost as if they had a life of their own. Once they're out in the open, the relief is immediate. Without waiting for an answer, Cathy leaps up, quivering, and scurries away.

In the forests of Shivering Heights, summer gives way to fall. There are no fires, but the air is smoky, as if the leaves would rather burn down to ash than dry up. The river exhales an icy mist.

Along the riverbanks, Cathy feels her nostrils throbbing of their own volition, slender membranes tensing up and then relaxing, tensing up and then relaxing. She is startled by the sights around her: a white moth, an immaculate inflorescence in the heart of a bush, pale larvae writhing on the ground. For days now, fleeting shadows have troubled the edges of her field of vision. They sneak up on her when she least expects them. Whiteness in any shape or form now looks suspect to her, a potential breach in the land of the living. She has lost the ability to distinguish animals from their shadows, the living from the dead, human sounds from the scratching and murmurings resurrected in the dark.

It was here, on these banks, that she first came upon the rabbits. In the warm air of early summer they were lapping up the stagnant water. Even then they had begun eating the insects in the grasses near the forest. That scientist obsessed with the river – Laura – watched over them by day. At night they took their chances with the foxes and wild dogs and unrecognizable poisonous berries.

From the moment Cathy brought them to the house, the Ogress began sizing up their fat paws, fleshy flanks, and silky silver pelts. Apart from their uncharacteristic taste for meat and a certain readiness to bite, they were a picture of charm: quick-witted, lively, joyful.

Cathy bites her nails and chews on a long blade of grass, and then another. She must find the perfect revenge. All attempts up to now have failed. Last night it happened again: before leaving for the costume ball, she sat at the dinner table in a Bunny costume: long rabbit ears, tights, bathing suit with a large white pompom, high heels. Minutes later, the Ogress approached with a casserole straight from the oven. She gave her daughter a sustained glare, then dumped the steaming-hot food on her. Cathy had to run her red skin under cold water for several minutes to stop the blistering.

She spits her blade of grass to the ground.

Vacationers have left their indelible mark on the riverbank: smashed beer bottles around a firepit, foil chip and candy wrappers, forgotten jewellery. Cathy's face, eerily pale, stares back at her. The wind carries the river's gurgling and something else, suddenly clear and defined – the sounds of human movement.

A few rocks away, perched like a bird on the shore, Laura is filling test tubes. Swaddled in a bundle on her back, a tiny creature squirms and cries hoarsely. Without letting her concentration falter, Laura plunges gloved hands into the cold river and then pulls them out again, laden with glass vials. She holds them up to examine in the sunlight, then places them in a cooler.

When Cathy approaches, she sees the samples lined up in the cooler alongside bagged specimens: frogs, garter snakes, and field mice, freshly collected, their bodies still warm.

'The rabbits are dead,' she says. She doesn't bother with a *hello*.

She feels a shiver creeping over her face and nerves throbbing between her nose and upper lip. Laura stares at her. This woman has perfect eyes, the kind you see only in aqueous dreams: twin golden orbs like portals to some other, deep-yet-limpid realm.

'I'm sorry,' Laura answers.

Her face clouds over.

'I know you were attached to them. Drinking this water wouldn't have helped them, unfortunately.'

Laura points at the river with her chin. Since early summer she has been gathering dead animals along the riverbanks in the hope of flushing out this evil that has them in its thrall. Someone has to. No matter the cost.

'Before they died … did the rabbits scratch you?' she asks gently.

Cathy has stopped listening. She's absorbed with a new idea. Her heart races; her entire being quivers. She can feel the landscape filling up with white silhouettes, fading into luminescence. Without answering the question, she snatches one of the dead frogs from the pile in Laura's cooler and flees. Between her fingers, its guts ooze out into the plastic sachet. She doesn't turn around.

❧

In Shivering Heights, even in summer, the sun's rays never fully penetrate the moist air or thickets of fir, spruce, maple, and ferns. At the forest's edge, people's yards become fens, fermenting the damp in a churchlike darkness; mosses and mushrooms cling to the sides of wooden houses the moment their spores are borne aloft by wind or mist. Windows here never quite get clean. No matter where you look, there is always a twig, or an earwig, or some growth of mould to remind you of outside.

Cathy lurks in the backyard, taking care to remain in the shadows of the trees. But her other senses give a clear portrait. Things she failed to notice mere hours ago become apparent. Even from outside the house, she can smell the peach-scented bubble bath the Ogress uses on evenings of amorous encounters. The taps in Shivering Heights never fully stop dripping, and the water carries a hint of mountain dust and an afterscent of limestone that only great mounds of foam could hope to mask.

When she finally goes inside, Cathy pretends her good mood has returned and goes to greet the Ogress in her bath. Then she discreetly lays her gift on the ground. The frog's belly is distended with post-mortem gas.

The slightest touch of the Ogress's foot when she steps out of the bath will cause the belly to burst into small, putrescent strips.

❧

In the refuge of her bedroom, Cathy waits.

When she hears the menacing thump of approaching footsteps, she slides her teeth along her nails. They taste of rot, muck, and seaweed, new flavours she finds delectable. Honed by weeks on a steady diet of next to nothing, her body has grown taut, ready to pounce. She feels nervous but powerful.

True, her nose is increasingly alive with palpitations. True, the uneasy thrill of confrontation is seizing her nerves and muscles and heart, making her lungs pump. But this feels like a necessary, natural state. In a corner of the mirror, a white gleam appears, trembling with life. She can almost hear the foot tapping.

When the Ogress darkens Cathy's door, she doesn't say a word. She is bathed, dried, and made up, in a black dress and a leather jacket with a rabbit-fur collar. In her hand is the frog with its gut busted open. A sprinkling of tiny arthropods covers its dangling entrails and fall to the floor along with drops of soapy water.

In through the window, the wind carries whiffs of their neighbours' barbecues and the fires being lit by Cathy's friends, who toast marshmallows instead of plotting revenge. For a moment, the teenage girl imagines the Ogress will force open her mouth and shove in the fetid batrachian body, for the pleasure of watching her chew on the infected meat until death intercedes.

This twilight is of the exact shade as the evening Cathy's mother approached the rabbit cage. The day she caught Panpan, as if to tickle her in that special spot between her floppy ears. In the reddish light, the rabbit hung from her right hand with its muzzle pointed down. The confused look didn't leave its face until the implacable Ogress clubbed it with the shovel handle. By the time Cathy realized what was happening, the butcher's knife had severed the carotid artery. Cathy stood paralyzed, unable to do anything but stare at the tiny animals left hanging from the clothesline for the better part of the afternoon. They looked like freshly washed stuffed animals, tied to the ground by a stream of thick burgundy blood. Then the Ogress hacked off their fur and turned the skin out, like the lining of a glove, revealing flesh of the same pink as Cathy's childhood bedroom.

The frog now hangs from her mother's hand in a way that recalls the rabbits, a bloody mass of dark shapes brought to the kitchen to be eviscerated.

It falls to the ground with a slurp.

'I've had it up to here with your shenanigans!'

The Ogress slaps her daughter. The sound rings out.

Instinctively, Cathy bites her.

That night, the taste of her mother's blood in her mouth feeds Cathy's rage. Her limbs tingle as she tosses and turns, trying to bite her own fist. When the white spots disappear, when her nerves have settled for good, when she can finally stop gnashing her teeth and tapping her foot: then they will fight for real. She'll bite and scratch and throw her prey to the ground, Cathy tells herself, immobilize her until she's no more than a moaning lump on the floor. As she prepares to drift off into violent dreams, she hears music beginning.

Little jaws are grinding; a paw taps out its nervous signals. The time of the apparitions is here.

Cathy gets up with a start. On tiptoes she crosses the room invaded by the melody of noises and gnawing, staccato clawing. She opens the door. Her nostrils are dilating and contracting in a nervous movement.

'Go forth, my little bunnies.'

They gather into a powerful flock, a rippling swarm. Cathy follows the sound through the house to the kitchen. Soon she can hear the rabbits chewing, leaping, and clawing away. Metal pings; chairs and floor squeak. They snuffle and sigh and yelp and occupy the space, leaping onto counters, climbing onto the window frames.

With a swift, assured movement, Cathy opens the Ogress's bedroom door. They hop toward it, flattening their thin rodent bodies to slip through the narrow opening, and then, one after another, they disappear. They are so light and cloudlike that only the faintest clicking on the linoleum can be heard.

Cathy leaves them to their work and cuddles up in her soft bed. Curled into a little ball, she scratches her feet against the sheets to mould her nest to the shape of her body. At last it is over. She lets herself be lulled to sleep by the nibbling sounds of the animals and the muffled groans of her mother that reach her through the cardboard-thin walls, until they fade as one into silence.

DEVORARE

She appears when the lights go out in cottage windows and the moon's rays expose the moths crouching on beds of leaves. The shrieks of rare birds pierce the sky, the scent of evergreens stings the lungs, and she advances, open-mouthed, through the labyrinthine forest.

The fog slips inside her like water through a fish's gills.

Her skin has the phosphorescence of creatures who dwell in dark caves, or feverish sick people sweating with vertigo. In heat waves and cool weather alike, a delicate mist forms on her forehead. She loves water. Cottage owners trade stories of coming upon her at night in some remote pool, swimming with a disconcerting ease.

Tonight she scrapes tree trunks for dust-grey lichen, then brings it to her lips. Its bitterness makes her grimace. She turns to a velvety moss, luxuriant as a fur coat, and caresses it with her fingertips before placing a morsel on her tongue. She can almost feel the tiny feather-like leaves disappearing in her throat.

She palpates her stomach, around the navel, where a scar traces a pink line.

Her body yields under her fingers' pressure. All the food in this forest could never fill the pit that has been dug inside her.

Heather's forward motion leaves no flower or mushroom untouched. *Pleurotus ostreatus. Hydnum repandum.* A fly spirals in a cloud of scent, then alights on her shoulder: she snaps it up, devours it. Anything that crosses her path is snatched and shoved into her mouth, her minuscule mouth, scarcely big enough to drain the albumen from a bird's egg. When the ripe scent of a plant reminds her of a sweaty body, she yanks it out and swallows it whole, down to its soil-covered roots.

On that night, along the road that cuts through the forest, Heather stops to salvage big hunks of roadkill deer. She puts them in a bag. Then headlights send her clambering into the ditch, where she rips open the bulrushes to savour their shoots.

She feels nothing but a slight pinching along her intestines while she swallows, chews, and then begins again. The bitterness rises up in her throat, but she holds it in. Hunger steals over Heather much the way pins and needles harrow the phantom limbs of amputees; it's a deeply felt, material wanting, an absence, a raging desire that cannot be slaked.

She massages her stomach, runs her arm over her mouth, then gets back on her way.

They say that, in the woods around Shivering Heights, certain species grow scarce. As some die out, others adapt with alacrity. No one can quite understand the foxes' adroit manoeuvres or the crows' suspicious looks. Different classes of insects are developing mutualist complicity. People are losing the ability to recognize living things once safely named, classified, and ordered into branches and sub-branches.

When Heather sees a small silhouette at the edge of a creek, she thinks she's found some never-before-seen animal, an unprecedented inter-species cross. But when she draws close and parts the ferns concealing the body, she recognizes that pointy face, those tapered ears, especially that long furry tail.

A squirrel. Its thinning fur has simply revealed more of its body. Its hairless paws have evolved into veritable hands, slender and sculpted. One might half expect this clawed, agile, lively creature to break into movement; one might half expect it to grab your hand and shake it.

She leans over and places her hand on the fur. It's still warm.

Heather picks up the squirrel with a surge of feral joy. Of all the dead animals she has come across on her feeding frenzies, never has she found one so perfectly fitted to her appetite, so wonderful, so predestined.

⁓

With a shovel, she smashes the window of a small cabin deep in the dark woods. She then sweeps away the shards clinging to its frame and slips inside.

Heather drops the dead animal on the kitchen table. It is still redolent of life, an almost rancid odour she notices as she draws it toward her. In her hand is a knife that she found in a drawer. Her excitement swells as she peels back the skin, uncovering a dark pink body of flesh so small and delicate it makes Heather shiver with pleasure.

She preps the squirrel and sets it aside on a plate. She'll roast it whole, so it arrives on the table still recognizable as the tiny, curled-up, delectable animal it once was. In the fridge, beside the usual eggs and milk and juice, she finds cut herbs, spring onions, even an almost-full bottle of wine. Her hosts are foodies. Heather smiles.

She turns on the oven and roughly chops garlic cloves. While the squirrel roasts, she cuts the bouncy deer flesh into small chunks, breaking to take swigs of wine or snack from the cupboard or lick the meat juice from her fingers. A moth comes in through the window and perches on the wall, astonishingly calm despite the artificial light. She grills it. Were she to stuff her face until her stomach's contents overflowed her throat, there would still be no quenching this hunger.

Tingles traverse her body; cramps stab her stomach.

Fragrant scents suffuse the kitchen.

Heather eats entire kilograms of deer, cooked blue, pulled from the pan the moment they sizzle. By the time the meat roasting in the oven is done, she is already full. She grits her teeth and keeps eating. She must not stop, especially now. She must cultivate a hope of plenitude. With every passing minute, the world outside Heather contracts while her insides swell. Yet the more she eats, the more her body seems not to fill up but to dilate, as if it were becoming the forest where animals dwell, or the great empty swaths of sky above its corpse.

When she sees the squirrel on her plate – a small round ball with tiny paws spread out like the still-unformed limbs of a child, and long slender fingers – she can't refrain from grabbing it with both hands, taking a deep sniff, and licking.

She trembles, closes her eyes, bites in. For as long as she has been alive, Heather's stomach has demanded she take the lion's share, whether she's eating lichen, cambium, fruit, leaves, insects, garter snakes, or deer. Never-ending is her quest to fill the void inside her.

The pain in her stomach makes her lean over and retch up her meal. When she tries to stand up, a thundering pain rocks her, and she drops to the floor on bended knees. Though her body begs to differ, she feels like a hollow tree or empty cave.

That night, she is gone before the owners come back to find the carnage that they'll put down to raccoons and coyotes, at least until they see the dirty dishes and empty bottle. In the forest, she walks with a limp. She alone knows the suffering born of this gaping hole in her abdomen. She alone can find nothing to satisfy her hunger among the bitter leaves and fruit hanging on the highest boughs, misleading mushrooms and tiny insects and small leaping mammals.

For the first time in ages, tears well up in Heather's eyes. Tonight it won't happen. Another night will go by without feeling, even momentarily, the weight of another body in the hollow of her own.

The weight of her twin, devoured in the womb, *fœtus in fœtu*, whose remains were ripped from her side.

URSUS MARITIMUS

Cold has no smell. It creaks and crackles and hisses, whirls the wind itself and people's cries for help, but no scent sticks to it.

Bundled up like an astronaut, Laura runs through the frozen air, inhaling and exhaling huge puffs of emptiness. She feels the green night blowing down to her fingertips. The northern lights ripple the fluorescent sky and she moves forward, weightlessly, toward the edge of the world.

Since landing in this town, she's been haunted by the austerity of the landscape. The houses agglutinating on the rocks, seen from the corner of her eye, look like shipping containers – spartan yardless cubes with tiny high windows. Vehicles lifted to handle epic snowfalls and adventure sit parked in front, awaiting their next mission.

In this wide open northern space, everything is small and all purchase uncertain. Moss, lichen, and even sound don't rise up normally but instead cling to the ground for a time before blooming forth in long slow waves.

Laura turns left at the end of the main road. She then goes straight for fifty metres, breaks into a sprint, veers left again. Her chest, stomach, and overoxygenated head float lighter with each step.

Then, without warning, the road dead-ends. Town recedes into tundra: the uninhabited tip of the continent. A gaping hole of emptiness engulfs this land, free of relief and devoid of trees. The final marker of human presence is a horizontal cylinder of fencing large enough to enclose ten men, standing a few dozen metres from the houses. A sign: Polar Bear Surveillance Program. Laura walks over, suddenly tiptoeing. Inside she sees only a shapeless, odourless hunk of meat. She bends forward with her hands on her knees, breathes a little, then slowly sets off homeward.

In the house Laura has rented, the owners' dog, Spooky, leaps up to greet her. He follows her into the kitchen to claim his share of her protein bar, and then into the bathroom where she turns on the tap to run a bath. Since she first set down her suitcase, this animal has scampered after her with a perkiness she finds at once irksome and endearing. She sometimes feels as if he were put here to remind her of her maternal obligations, a sentinel of what awaits when she returns. She throws the dog a ball and turns on the TV, then closes the door behind her.

Every night the bathroom becomes Laura's isolation chamber from the effusive affections of her canine roommate. These few square metres of smooth, uncluttered surface on which she lines up her collection of creams and serums is enough to take her out of the world. When she sinks into her ritual bath and the steam enfolds her face, she immediately feels her muscles relax.

Then, slowly, as the soap bubbles dissipate, her body appears under the water. Her breasts are scored with slender silver stretch marks, her stomach is a pouch of loose skin, her thighs are streaked with dilated veins like blue tentacles. All the kilometres she runs may add muscle mass to her legs and torso, but they can't do anything to compensate for the gradual weakening of the collagen in her tissues. She pinches herself to test the elasticity of her epidermis, palpates her varicose veins, methodically exfoliates.

The slightest abnormality alarms her.

In the bathtub, skin grown pallid in this northern summer relaxes, softens, and settles into creases.

Then she lifts a hand to scrutinize. Its bones have grown pointy, the protuberant veins are swollen from the torrent inside. This hand, formed almost forty years ago, is more and more craggy, like those of her mother and grandmother.

This hand portends a terrifying future.

It's strange, she thinks, with her hand in the air, that she has no memory of puberty. She cannot recall the first sprouting of hair between her legs, the twin mounds growing on her chest, the first time she noticed the tangy smell of her sweat while playing sports. Maybe the onset of sexual maturity seemed like no big deal amid the collective hysteria of friends and brothers and the other young people going through it along with her.

Lately, though, she's been intrigued by her own body. When the disturbing bulges started appearing on her hand, she began spending long hours in front of the mirror. She has been taking daily photos of herself, memories of her shoulders, legs, and feet. Once the transformations took hold in her tissues, she began her hunger strike.

She smears herself with opaque creams before lying down on her bed, arms stretched out alongside her body.

That night, new follicles appear on the tips of her shoulder bones. They are coarse and perfectly aligned.

From downtown, it's only a short car trip to the heart of the kingdom of the polar bear, *Ursus maritimus*.

'Don't lock the door,' says Laura's guide, Nathan. 'We'll have to be able to jump back in quickly if we get chased.'

'You sure know how to make a girl feel comfortable.'

She smiles at him. He hasn't changed a bit since the last time they saw one another. They've left town via a road that skirts the massive bay, bordered with rocks as round as the backs of sleeping animals. Summer is already over – such summer as they have this far north, that brief burst when the snow melts and lichen and brambles proliferate. They drive along the edge of the shimmering blue water where walruses and narwhals bask. It's still too early for bear sightings, they'd warned her, but you may see a few eager ones, out searching for patches of early floe, or ready to feed after months of fasting.

'It's great to see you again, Nathan.'

'Yeah. Never thought our paths would cross again.'

The friendliness in his voice tells Laura he isn't judging her for coming here. When he worked in her lab, she was drawn in by his contagious calm – that calm that over time helped ease her anxiousness at being a single mother, and her anger at the public indifference to the slow death of their world. So when she began looking for somewhere to flee, fearing the changes to the climate and on the surface of her skin, and the knowledge that her research could never be enough to save all that needed saving, she thought of that remote place where he had gone to pursue his research. She remembered his candour. They had been out of touch for years. And so she'd parked her son with her mother and left everything behind.

Nathan takes a few steps forward. They stay close to the car, ready to jump back in at the slightest threat.

'The pack ice is forming later and later in the season,' he explains. 'When the bears get hungry, they have a hard time finding seals. Sometimes they'll turn on us. We're right in the middle of their territory. It's happening more and more often.'

He grabs the binoculars hanging from a strap around his neck. The wind tousles his hair and reddens his milky-white skin as he observes the shore. He looks like he's never lived anywhere but this land of cold and rock. Laura wonders if the workers and adventurers and locals ever really get used to the dark and the isolation, the inhuman scale of the elements that life clings to like a speck of dust, or the disordered flow of time, which seems at once arrested and infinite, fugacious as a beetle.

They sit back down in the car to wait. In front of them, a white sun floods the tundra without warming it.

'There's one. Over there,' says Nathan after a while.

Laura turns her binoculars in the direction he's pointing. A silhouette moves slowly onto the rocks. It stands firm on thick, wide paws, its triangular head gently nodding in the sunlight. The transparent hairs of the *Ursus maritimus* repel sunlight while capturing the ultraviolet spectrum, warming the black skin concealed under fur. The bear's predatory grace is rooted in millennia of slow, circumscribed evolution, and a violence so ancient it cracks the surface of the present. A magnetic excitement pulses through Laura's stomach. Shivers lap at her legs. They should have eaten before coming here. Laura is overwhelmed by sensations she can neither outrun nor suppress.

'One thing I always tell tourists,' Nathan begins, 'is that some polar bears really will hunt humans for food. Not like sharks, who get a bad rap.'

Without answering, she pushes her binoculars tighter against her eyes. A discomfort steals over her body. Her hands begin to shake.

The bear clambers from rock to rock, unhurriedly. Even protected by the car's chassis, Laura still sinks down into her seat as she stares at it. She wishes she could be like the bear: a perfect replica of her ancestors, oblivious to the passage of time, with no vocation but following the rhythms of winter fasting and summer gorging on abundant purple-fleshed seals.

'I don't feel so well,' says Laura.

The bear turns its head toward them, then the landscape fractures into an avalanche of white points.

~

It all began with her hands. Her left hand, to be precise, on the table next to her glass of beer. The air in the bar smelled of popcorn and cheap draft. A thousand things competed for Laura's attention: the harangue of the activist speaking into the microphone, the sound of clammy hands applauding, the posters on the wall announcing demonstrations against the upheaval of the climate, the species, the entire geological order. The previous night had brought news: three new outbreaks of the parasite she's grappling with. But all she could see was that hand on the table – her hand. Of course, it was still what you would call a hand – metacarpal bones connected to five fingers, covered with skin, as it was before. But the blue rivers now visible in the region of her wrist were swelling as they flowed toward unusually pointy joints. Then there was the bandage around her thumb. That morning, the bulges she had seen swelling up had grown larger. Laura was horrified. She tried burning them with a match to stunt their growth.

All the disturbances of the planet seemed to be made flesh in her.

⌐∿

The sun has set and the greenish light of polar night shines through the thick glass, unsplattered with dead insects, pristine as a spaceship. Stretched out on the couch, Laura feels shivers running up and down her legs, back, jaw. Even something as simple as pulling the sheet up to her chin is enough to set her heart fluttering. Nathan rests his hand on her shoulder.

He has taken off her coat, but she wanted to keep her gloves on. He figures she is cold and doesn't protest. On the floor, Spooky sits calmly, staring at the television, where images of flying cars and bionic men parade by. She thanks Nathan with a smile. She's grateful to him for sinking into this silence with her.

Over the following days, Laura shuts herself in. She doesn't even answer when her mother's number appears on her phone's call display. She's almost stopped bothering to charge it. She unplugs her computer. Turns the television toward the wall, pretends civilization is at an end, walks around in the half-day of electric lights, her feet guided by a new-found lucidity.

It's said that sick and wounded animals instinctively begin to fast. Now Laura is fasting, not to combat the unsettling changes transforming her body but because she feels a certain justice in the act of deprivation. Her entire being is demanding to be regulated, brought to a standstill by the cold. Her internal mechanisms are slowing, her intestines calming, her heart rate moderating itself; each of her organs is expelling its last fluids.

Emptied of food and humours and thoughts, she transcends gravity and its weight.

Like the town, which, as the cold sets in, grows increasingly chalky and finally turns completely white, Laura too is leaving behind the luxury of temperate climes. Her curves are deflating into acute angles, the flow of blood between her legs drying up, the muscles sculpted by running being slowly ingested to fuel her system's greatly reduced activity.

She pretends not to see the little bumps forming all over her, swelling up, growing sharper and longer and stiffer until finally a slender white shaft with the consistency of a fingernail emerges.

When Nathan asks what's making her so anxious, she tells him that she can feel human time speeding up inside her.

One morning, staring out at the landscape through the window, Laura has a vision. She feels the sun and the moon blinking, faster and faster, as if the earth's rotation has sped up and days contracted to mere hours, minutes, seconds. The sun seems to cross the sky at breakneck speed, illuminating for only fleeting periods the settlers and the Inuit and the huskies that never stop barking. In the buildings, windows light up and then go dark again, and a steady stream of ships pull into and out of the bay. The children playing hockey in the street age in fast-forward. Laura has found the secret to seeing how the townspeople are born and die by the hundreds, like the crackling of some eternal fire. She too is wrinkling up, shrinking at an alarming rate. The hair on her head grows white while the hair on her body falls out; her skin now hangs flaccidly on her hands, like an old woman's. Her bones grow porous. The force of change spares only the most immense, inanimate things: sky, water, rocks people still stubbornly cling to. She sees roads being built and disintegrating, once and then a hundred and a thousand times, slithering like garter snakes in the deserts of snow. In the distance, along the bay, are the bears. *They* are the same as before – though not entirely. They were here before the arrival of the humans, and they will surely still be here after, when the houses lie abandoned, quaint artifacts of the Conquest of the North. She sees houses settling and sinking into the earth, sprouting holes and falling to pieces, inhabited now by the white animals of the tundra that will grow less white over time as the winters shorten. The time will come when no buildings remain; all will be fully absorbed into their surroundings. Other things too will have changed. Bears will have twin sexual organs; darker in colour and reduced in number, they'll feast on abundant prey in winter and summer, a new summer that will stretch out like the shadow of a sun that slips by between two green nights. It's a nauseating spectacle, as the water of the bay swells with a brilliant blue spreading all around like napalm, enthusiastically flooding everything the people around here have fallen into the habit of calling 'their land.'

Then, as fast as it appeared, this vision is gone. The landscape is itself again. Even the odd snowflake drifts down.

Cold has no smell. It creaks and crackles and hisses, whirls the wind itself and people's cries for help, but no scent sticks to it.

Bundled up like an astronaut, Laura runs through the frozen air, inhaling and exhaling huge puffs of emptiness. She feels the green night blowing down to her fingertips. The northern lights ripple the fluorescent sky and she moves forward, weightlessly, toward the edge of this world.

Tonight, for the first time since she started running again, she feels herself driven forward by a physical energy, as if her body has finally come out of its shell, definitively abandoned the horizontal plane to regain its biped state. Or maybe she just ate her entire dinner for once, she thinks with a smile. Nathan didn't say a thing, but watched her with a sense of wonder, like a man observing an animal devouring its meal at the zoo. Laura didn't mind. She even petted his hair, like a cat's fur. She turns left, and then heads off toward the community centre.

All around, in the secrecy of private homes, human life goes on in insulated pouches of warm air, as few and far between as the seals and walruses that will soon disappear under a layer of ice. The green night is deceptive, like the mirrored surface of the bay, like the frozen ground cracked by the cold. She takes a left, and then a right. Laura enjoys watching the town being tucked into the tundra's silent night, before sleep comes.

It's the silence that makes the growl seem so loud. Laura immediately knows what it means. She picks up her pace and tries to move silently, in vain, of course. She can't resist looking back.

She sees the bear's upper body over the garbage bin. It has lacklustre fur, a black muzzle. Like an athlete, the bear is stretching its jaw muscles in preparation for the contest to come.

Her heart is going to explode. There is no doubt in her mind that the pressure will pulverize her organ, set a fire inside her. She runs as fast as her legs will carry her. It's a kilometre to her house. She can't think. The bear follows behind her, heavy footsteps squeaking in the snow. The bear is faster. She's light, with a pounding heart, and dreams of escaping into the air, but the only possible escape is along the horizontal plane. After a few hundred metres, she climbs into a car and immediately locks all the doors.

She is trapped.

In a matter of seconds, it's back. The bear sizes Laura up through the windshield. It is terribly gaunt, clearly starving, opening its carnivore's jaw so wide Laura can now see its sharp teeth and outsized black tongue. It prowls around the vehicle a while, smacks it with a paw, makes sure Laura is still inside.

In the car there's no way to call for help, attack, or otherwise survive. Except the horn. She honks. The bear begins furiously clawing the windshield; she decides to get out the passenger side. The moment she jumps out, the windshield shatters into a thousand tiny shards. The explosion gives her a few seconds' head start. Laura has the advantage of knowing the route. She formulates a thought: she must take her turns at the last minute, to throw this great mass of fat and muscle for a loop.

She wants to cry out, but the windows that ten minutes earlier shone with life are now as dead as a herd of seals on the pack ice.

As expected, the bear is slowed by its own weight at every turn. Her heart jumps when her ears tell her the bear is no longer alone. She now has two giant creatures on her tail. Digging into her deepest reserves of bodily strength, Laura pushes herself forward, cutting through backyards. She reaches her home a few dozen metres ahead of the bear. Spooky comes out when she opens the door, she can't stop him.

She grabs her phone and feverishly dials the Polar Bear Watch Brigade.

Through the window she sees Spooky trying to change direction. Under the lamps, two white shapes watch him. He's too slow. With a single blow, the first bear pins the dog down on the ground. He claws off big hunks of flesh that swiftly disappear between his jaws. Like the snow, his body is splattered with blood. The first bear turns toward Laura, like a clot breaking free from the landscape, while the second one picks bare Spooky's remains.

In the kitchen, Laura grabs the biggest knife she can find. She knows full well that, even in its starving state, the bear has stores of strength that she can never hope to match. She takes up a post in front of the window. The bears are closing in now. A cub joins them, along with a third, even more emaciated adult. *They're turning up earlier and earlier in the year*, she remembers Nathan saying. *Hungrier and hungrier. But sightings are still rare.*

Only a few metres and a fragile pane of glass now separate Laura from the melee. In their pupils there shines a dark instinct, the instinct of life that must take life to survive. The window is too high for them to climb up to, but just before the Brigade arrives to disperse them she is sure she sees something she struggles to believe: the smaller one, with the help of another's muzzle, has climbed on the larger one's back. They are making a ladder with their bodies. Laura squeezes the handle of her knife. The skin grows smooth around the joints, pulled tight by her instinct to fight.

Then, on her wrist, one of the rigid bumps that have been growing for a while begins to thrum, then splits open. A feather pops out. It quivers there: a spotted feather like a bird's.

Meanwhile, outside, the bears run in every direction, between the Brigade vehicles.

Dozens of vesicles burst all over Laura's skin. Out comes feather after feather, all oily and new.

They suddenly bristle.

Survival is eternal.

Every night, quakes in time's surface rattle the dreamer's mind. As monsters from beyond the tomb come flooding out, dreams trace the contours of what *Homo sapiens* dimly perceives as future threats. Populated with beasts and cataclysm, these dreams may consist of the memory of timeless fears, reminders of the frailty of the human body – this waterlogged machine that's yet so quick to drown, this predator so easily devoured.

Maybe what each person dimly apprehends is true: dreams are omens, created by and destined for human beings, a warning to ourselves from a space out of time.

The meanings of these elusive premonitions haunt the dreamer long after they open their eyes.

REQUIES

Fat translucent raindrops agglutinate like insect eggs on the glass, blurring the view. The eight men and women around the table are hopped up like a gang of teenagers. Some mock each other mercilessly, some scarf down this meal as if it were their last supper, drenching each mouthful in butter and cream, and others stare down at their plates with a palpable angst. Knife in hand, Alex gazes silently into the distance. The few who aren't hollering or stuffing their faces are staring out the window into a damp landscape that reminds them of the phlegmatic consistency of their own bodies beneath only a thin layer of skin.

They have long known they are protected by the armies of bacteria that colonize the pits of their stomachs. There was a time when yogourt commercials still made them laugh or, at worst, mildly uncomfortable. *Did you know there are more bacteria in the human intestine than there are people in the world!* Most had little trouble sweeping such information under the spotless rugs in their Scandinavian minimalist decors. Today, the thought of their inhabited stomachs, like the knowledge that the universe is expanding, triggers a nausea no pill can relieve. Just as it is hard to picture life developing light years away from their planet, the concept of matter becoming discontinuous on the cellular and atomic scales sickens them.

Like a ravenous sailor, Alex holds her knife perpendicular to the table, mainly to stop herself from turning it upside down, pointing the tip toward her skin, and plunging it into her body. The eight people gathered in this room are hyperaware of their bodies. Sometimes they spend pinched-lipped hours massaging their stomachs and staring out at the river as it overflows its bed. At other times they put every ounce of energy they have into reconciling their constituent parts. Then they slide into other people's beds and let out sighs, gentle exhalations warm and sweet as summer winds. Usually they can sense an energy, like the electrical charge that comes before a storm; it makes them want to run, and fight, scream at the seeping green sky and the filthy floodwaters. They are growing more agitated by the day.

There isn't much time left. When he notices Alex's posture, Lawrence leans against her shoulder, gently forcing the young woman to set the blade down on the tablecloth. He whispers something to her that the others can't hear, gives her hand a gentle squeeze, then gets back up again. He wants this touch to infuse her being, all the way to her heart. He wishes he could take her in his arms, take every one of them in his arms, make them forget the implacability of time and the permeability of their bodies. He wishes he could, with a single movement, normalize their breathing and blood flow and all the thoughts that haunt them.

In this frenzy, Alex's anxiety has gone unnoticed. To resist the urge to pick up the knife again, she sits with legs crossed and hands clasped, like a schoolgirl. She opens her mouth, as if some sound were waiting to come out, but soon shuts it. Then, without a word, she lunges forward. Her hands have ceased obeying her mind. Social niceties have fallen by the wayside. She spews up her meal all over her dress, with its gentle scent of laundry soap.

The room falls silent. Lawrence takes hold of Alex's arm and carefully sponges her clothes clean. Then nurse and dying patient get up together.

In the preceding days, the floodwaters had been closing in on their cabin like a trap. Even when the rains were at their most violent, the sick ones kept going outside – to run, to dance, to lie open-mouthed on the wet earth. They were no different then than they are now: furiously alive, exhausted, euphoric, convinced of their own ignorance and their ability to subsist at once in extreme excitement and the most profound fatigue, of their power to explode and to dissolve, like walking corpses or ecosystems on the verge of implosion. They had followed him of their own volition to this remote outpost – to mitigate the risk of contagion, escape the hysteria gripping the city, live out the last days before their extinction. The choice hadn't seemed irrevocable. Then they found themselves on an island, surrounded by water, stripped of any possibility of leaving. They're never going back.

Insects swarmed all around, but the animals they should have seen in these parts had been swept away by the floods. Only the birds remained, on perches high above the ground. From time to time they formed terrifying flocks and took flight, whirling around in the sky before diving back to earth. At the sight of this, some were visited by auguries of obscure purport and then left wondering whether they themselves – parasite-ridden earthbound mammals – might be prophets of doom. They asked question after question until they could no longer say for certain where their own beings ended or what lay beyond. Is it true that we are what we eat? Or are we rather what we breathe? The excreta and carbon dioxide and kinetic energy we pump back into nature? Were we really no more than the sum of our parts? Were we the clouds, the trees, the stones? If even microbiota were distinct from our organism, on a small enough scale, how could anyone say for sure where their own being stopped and the birds began?

Lawrence had never once lied to them. He cared for them, one and all; while they ran and screamed and cried and self-mutilated, he washed their clothes and cooked their meals. He gave them pills to ease their symptoms, made sure their rooms contained all they needed to rest in comfort. At the end of the day, they would fall into his arms and thank him for not forsaking them, for not building a raft to float away on. No one knew what lay behind his devotion, but all felt increasing gratitude. Some even found an unlikely levity. They would joke around before turning in for the night, let themselves gently drift toward the beds where they could close their eyes at last.

❧

Some might claim Alex left them after hours of acute suffering. In truth it was over in a microsecond, like the flip of a circuit breaker. She was there; then she wasn't. That woman who just yesterday had wielded her knife with a survivor's ferocity was now a lead-coloured lump at their feet. The world around them teems with life. In the river, in the puddles, under rocks, in every atom of the waterlogged earth in which they are digging a hole to lay their companion to rest. Worms, beetles, fungi, algae, viruses, protozoa. *Calliphora vicina*. Everything is inhabited: the sky and the forest, the river and the living soil whose every crevice overflows with water. Alex will not be buried alone; she will be laid in the ground with the agents of her own decomposition. They think about the foreign bodies living in her abdomen, the ones that constituted her for the length of the epidemic, and the period of quarantine out here in nature – long enough for the symptoms to mature, long enough for an ending. It's best not to read too much into it, they think, since the idea of her decomposing with these monsters enrages them. When they contemplate her, it's their own fate they see. They wish there was a way to rip open her stomach and yank out the interlopers, sew her lustreless skin together again, and slip one of her dresses onto her body. They hope against hope that in death we all become our one true, univocal self, but they know too well the opposite is true. Underground we just disintegrate. Each atom that made us who we were turns into something else – everyone imagines a tree or a plant or a flower. We'll just as likely return as a larva, or something equally repugnant and insignificant: a fungus.

In the group of men and women digging the hole, Lawrence stands out for his serene expression and smooth skull tilted toward the ground. But what truly sets him apart is his outfit and waterproof boots. Lawrence alone does not see his own future in Alex's fate; he alone is not bent double in pain. It is more a happy accident of good health than choice of profession that drives him to provide food and succour, to prop up cushions under their bedridden backs and place capsules on their tongues. When the river began its rise, no one worried about their supplies or how to get help. They already knew how the story would end. So they dig. They lay Alex's body in the hole and stare at her. The wind rises and falls without rhyme or reason, and the sky changes colour behind the clouds, shadows playing over the face of the person they came here to bury.

Though the corpse's cells have already begun to shrivel up and microscopic bacteria have set to work, the dead woman's features are so rigid that the group immediately notices the tiny opening between two pale, almost blue lips. They all see the hooklike thing slowly emerge from her mouth. It's the curved foot of a parasite. Petrified, they wait. Standing around the grave in a circle, they watch in horror as the creature's phosphorescent shell emerges from her body, then comes to rest in the dead centre of Alex's face.

The seven who remain exchange stupefied glances. Instantly and without discussion, they are of one mind: the thing that came out of the dead girl after her extinction is no longer part of her. As one, they throw themselves upon this creature, a swarm of enraged, vengeful hands rushing to fling it to the ground, where they crush and trample it until nothing remains but a small purée of cells and fluids.

Over the following days, the most unsettling memory will be not Alex's demise but the emergence of the parasite. Lawrence will tell them the creature had no chance of surviving in the outside world. The literature is unanimous, every known case confirms it: the fate of the attacker is to die with its host. This knowledge does not stop the seven incurables from punching themselves in the stomach at night or from pinching their flesh in the hope of injuring the interloper within. Nor do these simple measures preclude others of spectacular futility, like making themselves vomit and then searching the toilet bowl for traces of tiny white crustaceans.

'I heard they pulled one from a man's stomach. Thirty centimetres.'

'When I go to bed, it feels like they're climbing up my esophagus.'

'I don't see how I can keep eating. I'll never swallow anything again. Never again.'

'I can't stop seeing its pale, slimy back. And those legs!'

'Stop, I can't take it. Just don't think about it.'

Like every other facet of their lives, their insomnia is collective. One night they discover they can no longer withstand the pins and needles in their veins. They come down from their bedrooms and meet outside, at Alex's burial site. Suddenly they are shivering. They imagine they hear whispers, murmurs, something moving through the curtain of foliage. Invisible insects dart all around; the river roars. Night is every bit as alive as day.

Stretched out on the ground, they defy the world to consume them. Some bury themselves under shovelfuls of earth, leaving only their heads above ground, quietly begging the maggots to eat them if they can. But after a while they start clawing at the topsoil, until they finally pull themselves out from the earth, panting and victorious. Others let dragonflies settle on their arms, shoulders, and heads, until someone else comes by to blow them away. They are so nervous and tired. It may be a collective hallucination when a long-haired naked woman emerges from the torrent and lays her spume-white body alongside theirs. *Now we are one*, she seems to say as she caresses them in turn, grazing skin and hair, gently rubbing backs, awakening desires. When they realize where she is taking them, they start to resist. They pummel her, scratch her. She just laughs.

Then she sinks her teeth into their skin and squeezes their wrists with force enough to cut off the blood flow. None can say for sure whether they are dreaming or awake. But in the end there is nothing so satisfying as an indelible pain that annihilates everything, and they know long before they see her return to the water whence she came that they have lost their bet.

They know it is her scream that rings out whenever rain falls in Shivering Heights.

At daybreak they find August, the oldest member of their group, lying in agony in the grass under pounding rain. He is curled up in a fetal position, holding his stomach with both hands. His eyes are rolled back in his head; his unnaturally stiff legs thrash against the ground.

Nearby, a container of water purifier lies on its side. It is empty.

He has ingested the whole bottle.

They all have the same look – eyes wide, fists in front of mouths – as they stare. August quakes and moans. They wonder what to do. They could take him to Lawrence, force him to swallow charcoal capsules, beg him not to die. But maybe the parasite's vile legs are at this very moment performing their final reflexive kicks under the effect of the chemicals. Maybe he has found the trick to expel them, to take them with him.

It's not as if they can leave him alone. But they can't save him either.

Soon they start dying in rapid succession.

They, the six survivors.

The five.

The four.

As they perish, one after another, they'll bury their dead in the ground or throw them in the river. Never have their surroundings been so alive. The water rumbles like an undernourished stomach. The froth on the surface of the pallid whirlpools is the spitting image of the clouds. Birds squawk and lunge skyward. Mosquitoes plow along like tiny zeppelins, surrounded by other unnamed insects. Such abundance of fauna, ignored all these years. They make a funeral pyre for the fourth corpse. It takes all day to get it burning in this damp air. Eyes on the flames, they brave the stench of burning flesh, hoping to see a crablike creature wriggling as it burns. By disposing of the dead, they seek the consolation of crushing one's enemies. They want to believe they are winning. In the ashes of the fourth one they find no shells, only fragments of bone, which bring to mind the particles they ingest with each deep breath. They cough. Bring hands to throats.

They're ensnared.

From the cabin, Lawrence watches them shovelling ashes into the river, then savagely beating the air with the shovel to chase the clouds of grey dust. From time to time, tears roll down their cheeks. He had hoped to ease their suffering, at least a little. But the sight of their rage as they incinerate their dead makes him wonder whether it was all for naught. Why help a few human beings among the glut of corpses that is on its way? Why try to appease the unappeasable? Maybe, before this last gasp of a dying civilization, there is simply nothing to be done. Exhaustion gnaws at him, the desire to give it all up steals over him.

Then he watches them topple over, and get up again, and keep on working. They have such need of tenderness.

So he gets back to washing their clothes, changing their sheets, preparing medications and meals. He sweeps up the feathers they have shed and brushes their dry skin, thin hair, and iridescent scales. Their stores of food are running very low. But only four remain. One refuses to eat. In a few days all will have succumbed to the epidemic. Then he'll leave Shivering Heights for the beleaguered metropolis. If the circumstances haven't changed, and if he takes sufficient precautions, perhaps he'll manage to bring a new cohort of the dying here, to help them live out their final days in a blanket of human warmth, far from the bedlam of the cities. Sometimes, before they squeeze out their last breaths, the men and women afflicted by the catastrophe shake his hand with a surprising vigour. He wants to believe there is solace in this hand of his. When one of them comes to him, ready to set out on their final journey, he tries to channel all his powers of comfort into his palm, before the current running through him disappears, before the energy he conducts dissipates, before the electric concentration of life gives way to a feeble death rattle.

These people too will know this peace.

These four.

These three.

These two.

↜

It's said the sky is blue and its light is what colours the water. But in this place, the misty air is fogged with greens and greys, hues running the gamut from matte to fluorescent. Hidden beneath the river's glimmering surface are countless creatures and an unprecedented threat born of recent climate change and millennia of evolution.

Seemingly oblivious to it all, the two remaining humans run as fast as they can along the banks of the raging river. Sometimes, when their focus is sharp, something unprecedented happens. Their feet leave the earth and, for a moment or two, they float, suspended in the air, ten centimetres off the ground. In this way they move forward, a metre or three, only to fall to the earth again. It doesn't stop them from trying afresh, again and again. The mother helps her son with a series of affectionate gestures. Wipes the dirt from his arms when he falls, runs alongside him while he gets moving again.

Lawrence stares in amazement. Every hair on his body bristles with joy, and his fists clench in hope each time they take flight.

'Keep going,' he says. 'Breathe! Flap your arms!'

Uncertainly, chaotically, their bodies rise. From time to time, when they attain a certain height and enter the flight path of dragonflies, Lawrence can see them growing lighter: they smile sweetly, blink more slowly.

Then they stop losing elevation. At first they glide in circles, above the ground, jerking like wounded birds. Lawrence watches, riveted. The world is no longer quite the same. The rain keeps swelling the foul river waters; the sky is still alive with biohazard colours – yet there they are: mother and son. They're flying. They start off in single file, then go side by side. They seem to communicate silently. In a single movement they break through the invisible wall separating the cabin from the rest of the world. They glide over the river's thundering torrents; the boy glances at the water's surface and then climbs a little higher, and soon they both disappear into the treetops across the water. Lawrence watches, enraptured. He is now the last man here.

He listens to the roaring river and the gusts of the wind that make the leaves whoosh and rattle the shutters. It's the wind after the storm. He is well and truly alone. Isolated amid the crows and maples and pines, the insects and billions of parasite eggs, biding their time, carried along by the river.

He takes one last look at the cabin, then slides into the water. The time has come to get back to wilder times.

FAUNA

In the dying embers of the night, there is a changing of the guard. Some living creatures fade into silence; others spark to life. While certain souls finally coil up and rest inside their skulls, cut off from the visible world, other eyes open. They are the yellow of wild animals, birds of prey, and other guardians of the night – the colour of suns in the darkness.

These beings have no name for forest. The meaning of woods and undergrowth resides in the slick or dry texture of tree trunks, the precise shades of green ferns at daybreak, the odours of rot or trails of slime left on them. Shivering Heights is no longer Shivering Heights for them. These foglands are in constant flux. One day the ground is soaked in water that leaves behind an acid taste, the next it's spotted with fat snow-flakes. Its serenity is pierced now by a howling wolf, now by a woman's screams.

On the carpet of crackling leaves, a small group of humans advances, careful to stray no more than an arm's length apart. In the dark palimpsest that is the forest floor, the traces of their passage are little different than those marking the presence of mammals or birds. They're recognizable also by their faint foot-prints, pungent body odours, and the lamplike glimmer in their glow-in-the-dark eyes. Their destiny can in no way transcend their raw materials: they will be born, and reproduce, and die. Their cells will be recycled.

While one woman gathers fir branches for their beds, the others forage. On the ground, small animals scurry by, barely visible, and burrow down, away from the human gaze. The creaks and breaths of night gently permeate the silence.

The sounds familiar to keener-eared, more attentive species are the same the woman strives to pick out when she's alone. But she can hear only branches creaking and snapping against her arms, her own footsteps and breathing, her beating heart and the bodily excretions between her legs as she squats before sleep.

She flies up to an unoccupied branch and, feet clenching the bark tight, closes her eyes a few moments. Up here, the murmuring of her fellow humans on the ground is little more than muffled ambient noise. The wind whistles in the leaves and in her hair, carrying with it countless cries and whispers.

On her branch, a caterpillar inches toward her. Sometimes, when she sees unknown beings, she feels an old desire welling up. *Name it. Classify the living.* But she has learned to contemplate instead – at least most of the time. Just as she now stares curiously into the iridescent reflections of this spongy, oscillating larva. New configurations of the old materials.

All around her a new world unfolds, teeming with furies and violence and beauty. True, the humans of this new time cleave to tarnished images of the olden days, now grown so faint their memories scarcely retain the trace. These days the great newness of it all has so enraptured and terrified them that more often than not they fall into a dreamless sleep.

In the misty forest, the deer prick up their ears to catch the sounds of the wolfdogs who have left behind their ball games for more nocuous entertainments. In the safety of their burrows, rabbits wait for night to pass. Clouds drift between ferns, birches, and balsam firs, concealing prey from predator. Worms and beetles perform their immemorial duties under rocks and fallen trees. In the secret depths of the earth, whole populations of new insects are kept warm in their eggs.

Stretched out on the ground, the humans murmur words from the Old Times before going to sleep. A woman and her child sleep curled together in the fetal position, while another keeps watch from her perch above. A garter snake slips through the ferns, oblivious to the fox hunting it.

All around, in the earth, on the undersides of leaves and in the hollowed-out trunks of trees, the wait is now over for all that lay dormant.

Everything is alive.

Author's Acknowledgements

I would like to thank Antoine Tanguay, publisher of Éditions Alto, for believing in this book and adding his formidable creative touch, and Karoline Georges, without whom I could not have pushed it as far as I did. I am grateful to Alana Wilcox for giving *Fauna* a new life in English, and to Pablo Strauss for his elegant translation. Thanks also to my early readers René Audet, Charlotte Biron, Mahigan Lepage, and France Plourde, for their comments at various stages; to the biologist Annie Langlois; to the wonderful Éditions Alto and Coach House Books teams; and to my friends and family for their unwavering support.

And thank you, Francis, for being marvellously supportive of all my endeavours.

Translator's Acknowledgements

Thanks to the author for her assistance, Mary Thaler for her insightful first reading, editor Alana Wilcox for her keen eye and staunch support, and the entire Coach House team.

Christiane Vadnais holds an MFA in creative writing, and has long been active as an events programmer and project manager in Quebec's literary community. Radio-Canada named her a 'Young Author to Watch' for 2020. *Fauna* is her first work of fiction. She lives in Quebec City.

Pablo Strauss's previous translations for Coach House are *The Country Will Bring Us No Peace, The Supreme Orchestra*, and *Baloney*. He is a two-time finalist for the Governor General's Literary Award for translation. Pablo grew up in Victoria, BC, and has lived in Quebec City for fifteen years.

Typeset in Arno and Anisette

Printed at the Coach House on bpNichol Lane in Toronto, Ontario, on Zephyr Antique
Laid paper, which was manufactured, acid-free, in Saint-Jérôme, Quebec, from second-
growth forests. This book was printed with vegetable-based ink on a 1973 Heidelberg
KORD offset litho press. Its pages were folded on a Baumfolder, gathered by hand, bound
on a Sulby Auto-Minabinda, and trimmed on a Polar single-knife cutter.

Translated by Pablo Strauss
Edited by Alana Wilcox
Cover design by Ingrid Paulson
Cover image ©iStockPhoto/Katrine Glazkova
Interior design by Crystal Sikma
Author photo by Maryse Cléro-Nobréga
Translator photo by Étienne Dionne

Coach House Books
80 bpNichol Lane
Toronto ON M5S 3J4
Canada

416 979 2217
800 367 6360

mail@chbooks.com
www.chbooks.com